I 0556661

Readers react to *Dead Man Lying*

Exactly what you want in a whodunit.—Mary Doyle, author of *The Peacekeeper's Photograph*

This book took me on a Hawaiian mystery, thrill-ride adventure. Though I consider myself to be exceptional at figuring out plots and story lines in mysteries, this story... not so much. The plot twists and surprises made me not want to put it down.—Lisa Jey Davis, author of *Ms. Cheevious in Hollywood*

I was drawn in from the beginning.—Lynda Filler, author of *Lie to Me*

What a great read. Just when I thought I knew who did it, Scott introduced another twist. I couldn't put the book down.—McNic Traveler, Amazon reviewer

Bury knows how to keep the story real and give up a few laughs while dropping subtle clues—Anima Giraldez, Amazon reviewer

A fast-paced, page-turning, who-done-it thriller. Full of twists and turns and a believable plot in beautiful Hana, Maui.—Sharon Scott

Scott Bury transported me to what felt like an authentic Maui—Roger Eschbacher, author of *Ghost Star*

Just when you thought you knew...Bury spins the plot in a new direction. Mystery-telling as it should be.—Eden Baylee, author of *Stranger at Sunset*

A great story, with twists and turns to the end. All will enjoy this book.—Ellen Oceanside, Amazon reviewer

Dead Man Lying

A Hawaiian Storm novel

By Scott Bury

IndependentAuthorsInternational.org

The Written Word

Dead Man Lying
Copyright © 2021 by Scott Bury
All rights reserved
Paperback edition
ISBN 978-1-987846-28-7

This is a work of fiction. All resemblances to any person, living or dead, or any institution are completely coincidental. No part of this story may be reproduced or used in any manner without the prior written consent of the author, except for brief quotations in reviews.

Published by The Written Word Communications Company, Ottawa, Ontario, 2021.

An Independent Authors International title.

Cover design by David C. Cassidy
Edited by Roxanne Bury
Proofread by Joy Lorton, The Typo-Detective

IndependentAuthorsInternational.org

To Toby Neal

Contents

Chapter 1:
Death scene

A hazy sun shone hot on two women standing on a rough low platform of volcanic rock. The air was heavy with moisture and the smell of wet soil, flowers and the unique, spicy aroma of Hawaii. Long fronds and branches hung low, weighed down by rain that had only recently stopped. Yellow tape strung from tree to tree in a rough ring around the platform drooped with the weight of the rain, too, obscuring the words "Police Line Do Not Cross."

The taller woman was fit, with shoulder-length dark blond hair and large green eyes. She wore the office-formal blue blazer, dress pants and shoes that broadcast "FBI." She leaned carefully over one edge of the eroded platform where some shifting in the earth below had opened a narrow gully. Its bottom was littered with lava boulders that matched those remaining on the platform. More fronds reached over its edges from the forest around it, as if they were also trying to see the bottom.

"It doesn't look that deep. Maybe ten feet," she said. FBI Special Agent Vanessa Storm's foot slipped on the wet rock and she took a step back. *Why didn't I put on my hiking shoes instead of these?* She thought about the Mephistos in her bag, back in the car. Her first trip to Hana had shown her the ruin that the rain coast could bring to fine footwear.

She crouched down on the platform, the heels of her hands at the crumbling edge, trying not to let her pants touch the rock surface.

"It wasn't the fall that killed him," Maui Police Detective Nalani Ferreira answered. "The coroner feels he was dead before he fell off the edge. That's his initial thought, anyway. It will have to be confirmed in the lab."

Vanessa looked down into the narrow pit again. "There's nothing to mark where the body was," she said.

"The morning rain washed it all away," Ferreira replied. "At this time of year in Hana, it rains every day."

"It looks like it," said Vanessa. The path from the compound of houses and other buildings cut like a tunnel through dense trees crowded against broad leaves that grew up from the ground, competing against vines that hung from unseen branches above. Vanessa could just make out the corner of one of the outbuildings far below. Hidden in the branches, birds twittered and peeped, and occasionally she could hear large drops of water hitting lower leaves on the forest floor. "Should we be standing on this? It being a historical artifact?"

"We really shouldn't," Ferreira answered. "The local Hawaiian cultural organizations are going to complain about it. But this is the only way to see the death site."

They stood on top of the remains of a *heiau*, an ancient Hawaiian temple. All that was left was an uneven platform of piled lava rocks, worn by rain, maybe twenty feet across. The creeping roots of the rain forest had eaten its edges. Vanessa eyed the side that had collapsed into the gully, wondering how big the ancient temple had been when it was built.

Watching where she stepped, Vanessa carefully made her way across the heiau, toward the path through the jungle back toward the house and other buildings on the estate. "Is that typical, a historical, cultural artifact on a private estate like this?"

Ferreira was right behind her. "It's unusual. This heiau was abandoned and forgotten centuries ago, and rediscovered only after Steve Sangster had bought the property. Now that he's dead, you can bet some cultural organizations are going to be making a lot of noise for it to be turned over to the government or a museum."

Vanessa paused at the edge of the forest to try to rub some of the dirt off her shoes. "Steven Sangster. I can't believe I'm investigating his death. Did you like his music, Detective Ferreira?"

"Call me Lani. Yeah, I had one of Steven

Sangster's albums as a girl. I loved trying to figure out the hidden meanings in the words. Did you like him, too?"

Vanessa could not repress a smile. "I was a big fan. I had all his old CDs—still do. But I thought the 'hidden meanings' thing was blown way out of proportion. I thought his songs were easy enough to understand. Still, I had a *huge* crush on him when I was 16. He was so handsome."

Lani smiled back. "The blue eyes and the square chin, huh?"

So this is the famous Nalani Ferreira, Vanessa thought, looking at the slender detective with her peripheral vision while appearing to study the heiau. She was small for a cop, but athletic, with beautiful big brown eyes and cheekbones that told Vanessa of mixed Asian and Hawaiian extraction. She had tried to tame her thick, dark hair, but the humidity of Maui's rain coast was bringing the curls even through the hair band.

"Is this where it happened?" said an unfamiliar voice. Vanessa and Lani turned, and Vanessa's shoe slipped again. Her knee buckled and she almost went down, but Lani's small hand grabbed her arm, steadying her. Vanessa was impressed. Lani was stronger than she looked.

Steady again on the wet lava, she looked up to see a short, balding man letting the yellow police tape down behind him.

"Don't the words 'Do not cross' mean anything to you?" Lani demanded, stepping toward the man.

"I'm Jeffrey Sangster. He—the victim...I mean, he was my father," the man stammered. He did not step back, but instead stepped closer, putting a foot up on the lava rock.

"I'm sorry for your loss, Mr. Sangster, but you still cannot step past the yellow tape."

The man scowled, straightened his back and puffed out his little chest, which did not protrude nearly as much as his belly. "Now that my father is—I mean, this is now my property," he said, but his voice did not match his posture.

"I'm not sure that's quite true, but even so, this is a crime scene, and you'll have to step back past the yellow tape," Lani retorted. She lifted the tape for him.

"It's so that no one inadvertently compromises the investigation," Vanessa offered, trying to make her tone conciliatory. "Please, step back."

"In-investigation?" he said, seeming to deflate. "I thought it was an accident?"

"We'll have to wait for the coroner's final report to know that," said Lani. She stepped off the heiau and took the younger Sangster by the arm, directing him onto the path back down the hill.

Vanessa was just about to step onto the path when a koa tree exploded. Wood chips flew through the heavy air and the sound of a shotgun rolled up the slope. Lani threw herself off the path, pushing the pudgy Jeffrey Sangster down. Behind her, Vanessa dropped to the ground and rolled, tearing her jacket on ragged volcanic rock. They held still, barely breathing, counting the seconds as the top half of the koa tree slowly toppled.

No more shots followed. Vanessa lifted her eyes above long, pointed leaves. She counted to ten before raising her head. She felt rainwater and shreds of wood on her face. She could see the corner of a building a hundred yards down the hill, but no shooter, no glint of low sunlight on a barrel, nothing but the suddenly silent rain forest of Maui. The birdsong had stopped. All Vanessa could hear was her own pounding heart. She made an effort to breathe.

No more shots.

"Agent Storm, are you okay?" said Lani from her hiding place among the trees.

"I'm fine, but my jacket is ruined. You?"

"I'm good." Lani rose to a crouch, extending her arms to aim a Glock toward the house, then down the path.

Vanessa drew her Walther PPK from its shoulder holster, checking in the opposite direction. "What about Sangster?"

"I'm okay," he called with a tremor in his voice.

Nothing. No movement other than dripping water. A single bird tried a tentative chirp. Then others piped in, too, and soon the forest's usual chorus returned.

But there was no more gunfire, no sound of people until they heard footsteps pounding up the path. A uniformed Hana policeman came into sight, gun in both hands, pointed down. "Detective Ferreira! Are you all right?"

"We're fine," Lani answered, rising to her feet and lowering her gun. She stopped scanning to scowl at the cop. "How did you let him come up here alone?" She tossed her head to where Jeffrey Sangster was slowly rising from the ground, wet and covered in leaves, soil and fragments of new wood.

"I'm not hurt," he said, voice still shaky. "Was that a gunshot?"

"Sounded like a shotgun," said the cop. Vanessa finally stopped scanning the forested hillside to take a look at him. He was young, fit, and tall. His light brown hair had a decidedly non-cop wave over his forehead. *Gilmour* was stitched across the right-hand breast pocket of his black uniform shirt.

"Well? How did he get up here alone?" Lani demanded.

Gilmour swallowed. "I'm sorry, Sergeant. I didn't see anyone come up this path. I've never even seen this man before." He glared at Sangster. "You'd better come with me."

"I just arrived here from Kahului," Sangster said. "We only found out this morning. I came—we all came as soon as I—we could."

Lani pointed down the path, and Sangster took the hint. Gilmour followed him, with Vanessa and Lani hanging back a little. Lani pulled a walkie-talkie off her belt. "Hana station, this is Detective Lani Ferreira, seconded from Kahului. I want a forensics crew to meet me ASAP at the Sangster estate."

A tinny voice, probably a woman's, came back. "The crew just got back from there, just now."

"Well, get them back here, stat, along with more uniformed backup. Someone just fired a shotgun at an FBI agent." She clipped the walkie-talkie back on her belt and followed the cop.

"Do you really think that shot was aimed at me?" Vanessa asked, bringing up the rear. Like Ferreira, she held her gun high, pointed up, at the ready as they made their way warily down the path.

"You, me or Sangster. It's impossible to tell now. But saying a fed was the intended victim will get their asses in gear faster."

Vanessa realized that her heart rate and breathing had returned to normal, but she couldn't help but look over her shoulder every few steps. Ferreira, on the other hand, appeared cool as ever. *What has she gone through that she's not even fazed from being shot at?* she wondered.

Vanessa remembered the stories about Lani Ferreira, how she'd been targeted and stalked by a Maui crime family that had murdered her father and sent death threats to her husband; how she had gone after the killers fearlessly until one was dead and the others in jail.

The kind of cop we all dream to be.

Chapter 2:
The family

The mansion was appointed in what Vanessa called "Hana chic:" dark wood floors and walls, bright floral upholstery, rattan tables and chairs. Two fans rotated slowly at either end of the ceiling. Big picture windows along one wall showed a wide balcony with patio furniture, and a view leading down the slope of Maui to the Pacific Ocean, shadowed by the sun that was going behind the volcano. On the horizon, dark clouds gathered again, promising more rain.

A colorful painting of a young Steve Sangster hung on one wall. Vanessa remembered seeing it in some news story, how it had been auctioned off for charity. Now it was back in the subject's home? Under it was a baby grand piano, the top closed. Beside that was an acoustic guitar on a stand, and above it, on shelves, sat a sophisticated stereo system. Tiny speakers sat on little brackets, bolted to the walls near the ceiling all around the room.

Vanessa surveyed the throng that had gathered at her orders. On one brightly colored sofa was the elder son she had met on the grounds of the estate, Jeffrey Sangster. A short woman she had been told was Paula, his wife, sat at the other end of the sofa. She looked to be in her late 30s, with long hair that was colored several different shades of brown from almost blond to almost black, and large brown eyes, clouded in a scowl. She wore stud earrings with diamonds and blue stones, not quite big enough to be gaudy. Between Paula and Jeffrey were three little girls, all under 10 years old, wearing nearly identical dark brown hair styled long, all in matching pink and black dresses. They looked up at Vanessa with big, dark eyes and sad, frightened expressions.

Standing beside the marble fireplace was a blonde—Sangster's current wife, Kathryn—wearing very tight white jeans, a black blouse that stretched across her breasts, and so many gold chains they made Vanessa's neck hurt. According to the FBI file, she was thirty years younger than her late husband, and an aspiring singer herself. According to the gossip magazines and TV shows that Vanessa never admitted to reading or watching, Kathryn Sangster was a talentless gold digger who married Steven as a means to launching her otherwise laughable singing career. Vanessa had never heard Kathryn's singing voice, so she reserved judgment. *She looks more angry than upset about her husband's death,* Vanessa thought.

Standing at the opposite side of the room, as far from Kathryn as possible, was another young woman. She was African-American with dark brown skin, an oddly old-fashioned hairstyle and thick, dark rimmed glasses. She wore the closest thing to a business suit that Vanessa had seen in Hana: dark slacks, mid-high heels and a light, short-sleeve blouse. She stood back from the rest of the crowd, arms crossed, her expression both scared and sorrowful. *This must be Isabel West, the personal assistant.*

Sitting together on a wide upholstered chair were Sangster's daughter, Janet, and a skinny, dark man. Janet had inherited some of her father's looks, like the bright blue eyes and thick, wavy hair, the wide chin and full mouth. Like her father, she made no attempt to dress up her looks. Neither makeup nor jewelry adorned her. Her thick hair hung, unstyled and unbrushed, just past her shoulders, and her bright blue eyes were dark and bloodshot. She wore yoga pants that did nothing to flatter her body shape, Vanessa thought, and a loose beige top.

The man beside her seemed bored. Tall and skinny, his dark eyes stared out the window toward the darkening Pacific. A pair of expensive sunglasses was caught in the brown curls on top of his head. He wore a stereotypical surfer's attire of tie-dyed t-shirt and board shorts, and flip-flops on his feet.

Vanessa checked the notes on her tablet computer, which she held against her midriff, but could not decide who the man was. Behind Janet, leaning against the back of the chair was a pudgy boy of about 12, playing a game on a smartphone. Beside him, an overweight girl of about 15, with long hair dyed three different shades of blond, stood staring down as her fingers intertwined and relaxed repeatedly. Janet's kids by two different men, Steven Sangster's grandchildren, Ben and Madison.

Sitting on the piano bench was a young Asian man. According to the file, that would be Josh Fong, Sangster's sound engineer. *Why was he staying at the estate now?* she wondered.

Beside the door was a large, grey-haired Hawaiian man wearing coveralls, thick gardening gloves hanging out of a pocket. That would be Kaholo Iolani, a longtime friend of Sangster who lived in one of the small guesthouses on the estate and looked after the grounds.

Then, she recognized someone she had not expected to see in this room. Sophia Keahi, the local historian and Hawaiian cultural activist that Vanessa had met the last time she was in Hana, investigating the kidnapping of a young woman. She was thin and tall, with grey hair that hung past her shoulders. Vanessa had never been able to guess her age.

The local cop, Gilmour, stood just behind Iolani, holding his police cap in his hands, grim face watching the group.

Vanessa was conscious of missing the local police authority. Lani Ferreira had directed a crew of local cops wearing body armor and carrying rifles to sweep the grounds, looking for the shooter and evidence, and then prepared a preliminary media statement.

Vanessa tried to pull together the ragged edges of the tear in her jacket and began the speech she had rehearsed in her mind. "I am Special Agent Vanessa Storm with the Maui Resident Office of the Federal Bureau of Investigation. The first thing I have to say is that I am very sorry for your loss. Later, I am going to be speaking with each of you individually, but for now, I just want to give you as much of an update as I can at this point in time."

Janet, the daughter, was the first to speak up. "If you're with the FBI, does this mean my father was was ... murdered?" She whispered the last word, her hand at her chin. Her daughter, Madison, gave a little cry and stepped backward, bumping into Josh Fong on the piano bench.

"There is no evidence so far to indicate that. The police were called in due to the unclear nature as to the cause of death, and the FBI was involved due to Mr. Sangster's high public profile and possible interstate implications. I am here formally to assist the lead investigator, who is Maui Police Detective Sergeant Lani Ferreira. She has come from the main office in Kahului for a few days for the investigation, and is making a statement to the media now."

"What's she saying to the media?" Jeffrey asked.

Vanessa flipped through screens on her tablet. She felt embarrassed to see only three media vehicles waiting to break the news on Steven Sangster. She found the media statement she and Lani had worked out together.

"'This morning, the body of Mr. Steven Sangster, American folk music legend, was found on the grounds of his estate on Maui, Hawaii,'" she read. "'Medical professionals were called immediately, but unfortunately, the coroner pronounced Mr. Sangster deceased at the scene."

She looked at the crowd before her. There were tears on Jeffrey's and Janet's cheeks, reflecting the dim light from the window.

Vanessa took another breath. "That being said, there have been some developments since Mr. Sangster was found in the forest. Specifically, someone fired a gun, probably a shotgun, at Detective Ferreira, me and Mr. Sangster," she nodded toward Jeffrey, "who against police direction came to the spot where the body was found." She realized her tone was sharp, even harsh, and that her pulse sped up when she thought about the gunshot.

"A gunshot? Is that why all these cops are swarming over the whole estate?" asked Kaholo Iolani, the groundskeeper.

"That's why. And I am going to speak to each of you about your whereabouts for the past twenty-four hours," Vanessa answered, still conscious of her harsh tone. She took a deep breath, hoping no one would notice.

"At least tell them to keep out of the gardens and not to stomp on the flowers," Iolani grumbled.

"Are you going to speak with the children, too?" asked Paula Sangster, Jeffrey's wife. Vanessa heard the hint of an accent. *Spanish? French?*

"No. We'll speak with any minors in the presence of at least one parent," Vanessa said. "Let me state now that no one here is a suspect in any way. We're just trying to gather as much information as we can."

"Does this mean there's still a shooter on the premises?" Jeffrey asked. Vanessa could see sweat on his forehead.

"We don't know. That's what Detective Ferreira and the other Maui officers are trying to find out." She scanned the room one more time and looked at her tablet. Someone was missing.

"Are you cops searching the whole estate?" someone else asked. When Vanessa looked up, she saw the skinny, curly-headed man beside Janet Sangster looking at her.

"Who are you?" she said.

"This is my boyfriend," Janet said.

Vanessa consulted her tablet again. "Kefir Steinberg?"

"I pronounce it 'Kiefer,'" he corrected her.

Then you're pronouncing it wrong, Vanessa

thought.

Motion out the front window caught her eye. A cloth-top Mustang dodged around the three media vehicles perched at the entrance to the access road before pulling into the already crowded driveway. A tall, slim woman with long dark hair got out, and two women jumped out of the media trucks to chase her. The tall woman easily outran them, reaching the verandah before the reporters could get to the driveway to shout questions.

Vanessa's breath caught in her chest. *That's Erica Harrison—Sangster's second wife.* Even after all the years since her marriage to Steven Sangster ended, Erica Harrison still had a fan base and could sell out concerts. Vanessa had bought one of her albums as a girl.

"Let her in," she said to Gilmour, who opened the front door.

Erica entered in a flurry of dark tresses and denim. She wore a flowing scarlet blouse and faded jeans with her trademark big belt buckle. Despite the lines on her face and the traces of grey in her black hair, she radiated energy.

"Is it true?" she cried out as soon as she was in the door, then scanned the roomful of the Sangster family. "Oh my God. I just heard when I landed in Kahului. I came as fast as I could." She came to Janet, wrapping her arms around her. "I'm so sorry. Steve asked me to come earlier, but I put him off. Maybe if I had been here—"

"It's not your fault," Janet sobbed, and the two

women cried together, rocking in each other's embrace. "Dad was at the heiau. He fell. There was nothing you could have done."

"Dad was just too stubborn," said Jeffrey from the other side of the room. Unlike Janet, he hadn't stood when Erica Harrison had come in.

Vanessa let the scene play out. She knew that Erica Harrison was not the mother of Jeffrey and Janet. That was the first Mrs. Steven Sangster, Frances Garcia. Apparently, the second wife had established a better relationship with Janet than she had with Jeffrey.

Eventually, Erica let Janet go and took a tissue from her pocket. She offered another to Janet, and after drying her face, hugged Janet's daughter, Madison, and then her son, Ben. She nodded at Jeffrey and Paula and ignored Kefir.

"Ms. Harrison, I'm Vanessa Storm with the FBI," she said, offering her hand. "Please, sit down. Officer Gilmour, would you get Ms. Harrison a glass of water?"

"I'll get you something stronger, Erica," said Kaholo Iolani. *He knows his way around the living room*, Vanessa thought as the groundskeeper opened Sangster's liquor cabinet and poured a shot of bourbon into a heavy crystal tumbler.

Erica went to Kathryn, the current wife, and hugged her. She responded stiffly, avoiding a kiss. Erica turned toward Kaholo then, who put the glass of whisky into her hand. She took a large sip and turned toward Vanessa.

"The FBI? Why are you involved?"

"Initially, as a formality," Vanessa answered. "But a half hour ago, as Maui Police Detective Ferreira and I were viewing the site where Mr. Sangster's body was discovered, someone shot at us." She was glad she kept her tone neutral, at last.

"And at me, too," Jeffrey spoke up.

Vanessa ignored him. "When did you arrive on Maui, Ms. Harrison?"

Erica took another sip of the bourbon before answering. "Steve wanted me to work on some new songs with him. I arrived this morning from California. I had just gotten onto the Hana Highway in that rental car when I heard on the news that Steven had been found dead."

"Mr. Sangster wanted to work on new songs?" Vanessa asked. *Unbidden, the melody to one of his hits, "We're Starting All Over," began to play in her mind.*

"He said he had some ideas, and wanted to record one last album," said Erica.

"Another unnecessary risk," Jeffrey said quietly.

Erica ignored him. "He sent me a few samples. They sounded good. He told me he wanted to rekindle that creative spark we brought to each other," Erica sniffled. "I was happy to help. It had been so long since we'd seen each other ..." Her voice trailed off and the tears began to spill again. Janet embraced her once more.

Vanessa turned away and addressed the rest of the people in the room. "As I said, I'm very sorry for your loss, but we must get on with this investigation. I will speak with each of you individually in Mr. Sangster's study, with the exception of children, of course."

"Don't we have the right to an attorney?" asked Kefir Steinberg, a sneer twisting his face.

"Of course, that is your right. But having an attorney present will take time. No one here is a suspect at this time. Anyone who is willing to speak with me may do so. If you want to call an attorney, you may do that also. But those are the only phone calls I will allow at this time, and no one here is to leave the premises until I or a judge says so."

Kefir Steinberg did not look happy.

Vanessa turned to the remaining person in the room that she had not yet spoken with. "Sophia Keahi. What are you doing here?"

"I came when I heard my friend had died," she replied, her voice even, her face impassive.

"How did you know he's dead?"

"He was a friend. Of course, I would know."

Vanessa knew enough about Sophia Keahi to also know there was no point in trying to pursue this line of questioning. "I will have to talk to you separately. Soon."

She looked at her tablet. "Wait. There's someone missing, someone named Mai. Who is that?"

"She's the cook," said Kathryn. "I'll get her." She disappeared down a hallway that Vanessa assumed led to the kitchen. A minute later, she reappeared behind a diminutive Asian woman with black hair tied into a bun behind her head. She wore an apron over blue pants and a print blouse, and kept her eyes on the floor.

"Are you Mai Pham?" Vanessa asked. The small woman nodded, still not looking at her. "You're Mr. Sangster's cook?"

"I cook for whole family," she said in a voice that Vanessa could barely hear. "Miss Janet, Madison, Ben, Keefer, everybody. Even Mr. Olanee." It took Vanessa a moment to interpret the last name as "Iolani," the groundskeeper.

Vanessa stepped closer to the small woman. She could see the tracks of tears on her cheeks. "How long have you been working for Mr. Sangster, Ms. Pham?" she asked, keeping her tone as gentle as she could.

Still with her eyes on the floor, Mai said "One year, two months."

"Where are you from, Ms. Pham?"

"Vietnam."

Vanessa stepped back. "That's fine. We'll talk, just you and I, later." Mai nodded and returned to the kitchen.

"Agent Storm? How long will this take?" Vanessa turned to Jeffrey Sangster. "It's just that, with my father...his passing, all his accounts are frozen until the death certificate is issued, and there are some important transactions that I need to make —on his behalf, of course, things we agreed on in advance. There are deadlines to meet, and as long as the investigation is open, I cannot carry them out."

"There's no way I can predict how long an investigation will take. Someone has shot at you, me, a federal agent, and a Maui police detective. So this looks like it may be a complicated case."

"But—"

Her phone buzzed. "Excuse me," she said, walking down the teak paneled hallway toward the kitchen.

It was Al King, her boss, the Special Agent in Charge of the Honolulu Division. "I just heard you've been shot at," he said, without preamble as usual.

How does he know, already? It's eerie. "We're not sure I was the target," she answered, pausing at the kitchen door. "I was there with the Maui detective in charge of the investigation, Lani Ferreira, and the victim's son, Jeffrey."

"What was a civilian doing at a crime scene?"

"Trespassing."

Vanessa heard her boss take a deep breath. "How are you doing?"

"I ruined a jacket, and I don't think these shoes will survive either. But other than that, I'm fine."

"Vanessa, this assignment began as a formality, but a shot fired at a federal agent makes it a lot more complicated," King said. Vanessa pictured him, sitting at his desk, cradling the phone against his shoulder as he flipped through pages on his desk, his jacket rumpled and his tie working itself looser. "I'm sending Terakawa to back you up."

Alan Terakawa was her partner in the Oahu office. He had not accompanied Vanessa to Hana because, as SAIC King had said, the whole thing appeared to be a formality, and there was an economy drive going on through the Bureau. Whenever they could save resources, they did so.

"I don't think that expenditure of resources is necessary," Vanessa said. She looked across the kitchen to wide sliding doors that gave a view of a broad lawn, surrounded by thick rain forest that rose up the side of Haleakala, Maui's southern volcano. Overhead, clouds thickened, making the afternoon darker than normal. "Alan has plenty on his plate already."

"Vanessa, leave it to me to decide how much should be on Alan's plate," King said. "It doesn't matter who the shooter was aiming at. He put a federal agent in his line of fire. I don't want any of my agents to be—" A short beep interrupted him, but King continued as if he had not heard it. The beep came again a second later, the signal that another caller was attempting to contact her. Vanessa let the call go to voicemail. "—vulnerable like this. Terakawa will be there as soon as possible.

"That being said," he continued, and Vanessa heard him sigh again. "The weather here has socked in all flights from Oahu to Maui, so you'll be depending on the Maui force for support until it clears up. Trust Ferreira—she's a good cop."

"Good to know."

"One more thing. Your training course deadline is coming up fast. You need to complete at least one more module by tomorrow. The system will notify me as soon as you do, and then I'll authorize you to go to the next level."

"Really? I have to worry about that now?"

Vanessa felt a headache brewing. Family conflicts and secrets made the Sangster case complex enough, without having to pile on stress from Human Resources.

"You signed up for it, remember?" King said.

"Can't I get an extension since I'm on an assignment, away from the office?"

"Sorry, Vanessa, I don't make the rules. You've had three extensions already. Look, just finish one more module after you knock off this evening, and I'll authorize it. Then, I'll be able to authorize another extension for the next level, but the system won't let me until you finish one more module. Okay?"

Vanessa sighed as her phone beeped again. She glanced at the screen at a text message. "Okay.

I'll do it tonight," *even though I hate online exams. All exams.* "I have my tablet and my notebook computer." She hoped her boss didn't hear her sigh.

"Good. I'll watch for the notification. And Vanessa?" King added. "Be careful. These celebrity cases have a way of getting more and more complicated." He clicked the line closed.

Vanessa sighed as she tucked her phone into a pocket. *It's going to be another late night on the computer.*

Chapter 3:
Evidence

"That is all the information we have at this time," Lani said, concluding the media statement.

She was disappointed and saddened at the poor turnout by the media. One was the Maui TV station's local affiliate, KHIN. Lani recognized the junior reporter, Aisha Chen, and wondered how someone so young could appreciate just whose death she was covering.

There was a freelancer she had seen once or twice before, sitting in the driver's seat of a rusty old Kia, holding a cheap digital camera and drumming his fingers on the steering wheel. The third she did not recognize, a man and a woman with off-island hairstyles and dress clothes. *Maybe some music website,* she thought.

It's really too bad. At one time, Steven Sangster was the American singer-songwriter. The new Dylan.

That was a long time ago, she had to admit. *Steven Sangster just doesn't command as much interest in the general media, anymore.*

On the other hand, she knew, Hana's

remoteness was another factor. It was just hard to get there. Which explained Aisha Chen's presence. Southern Maui was her beat, and she had probably been close by. And the freelancer looked like someone who spent as much time on a surfboard as on his computer.

"Thank you," she said, turning away from the small group at the bottom of the outside steps to Sangster's front door.

"Detective Ferreira, is there any suspicion of foul play in Steve Sangster's death?" asked Aisha Chen.

Lani was conscious of the KHIN-TV cameraman zooming in on her. This was the part of the job she hated most. Worse than paperwork. Worse than performance reviews.

Media statements.

Camera-shy at the best of times, Lani felt as if every blemish on her face would be blown up to huge proportions on TV sets across the island. And with a victim as a once famous singing star, her face could very well be on TVs around the world within a couple of hours. She was even more conscious of her hair getting further out of control every second in Hana's legendary humidity.

Then there were the questions, the reporters trying to trip her up, catch any inconsistency. She had to give them some kind of answer, without revealing anything confidential, anything that might compromise the victim's or the family's privacy and of course, anything that might not present the police force in the best possible light.

"We have no statement to make regarding evidence or cause of death at this time," Lani answered, turning to go.

"Is there any connection to the rumors of connections to drug trafficking in Maui?" asked the scruffy guy with the cheap camera.

He wore a bright Aloha shirt, cargo shorts and flip-flops. In other words, he dressed like just about every man on Maui, all the time.

This was what Lani had been dreading: a question that caught her off guard. She had heard nothing about any connection between Sangster and drugs, other than the singer's long-notorious love for marijuana, and his continued support for the legalization cause. But drug trafficking?

"Um, no, there is no connection," she stammered.

"Could that be because of the rumored connection between local police and the illicit trade in opioids in Maui?"

That rumor was something she had heard. But there was no way she was going to say that to the media.

Mr. Scruffy went into Lani's unfavorable category—a reporter trying to raise his own profile by looking for a link between the tiny stories he stumbled across, to the issues getting the most play on network television. Police corruption would be great for him. *Even though the relationship between police and the community is generally good in Hawaii.* "I have stated all the information we can share at this time," she said and turned away.

"Detective," interrupted the woman with the fancy hair and suit that was way too formal for anywhere in Hawaii. "Is there any truth to the rumor that Steve Sangster was about to release a new album?"

At least this is something that won't embarrass the force. "Again, we have no further information that we are prepared to share at this time."

She saw the crime scene investigation team standing at the corner of the house, watching her expectantly. Lani let out a sigh. "Now you will have to excuse me. I have to get back to the investigation. Please remember to stay behind the yellow tape. This entire estate is the scene of an official investigation."

Not exactly true, but close enough.

She ignored the perfunctory questions thrown at her back. Not like the scrums in cop movies, but then, there were only three reporters.

The head of the CSI unit was John Reid, a tall, slim man approaching retirement. He had driven down from the station in Kahului along with his assistant, a petite woman named Sheree Patel. Standing a head shorter than Vanessa, she was very thin with dark, dusky skin, big expressive brown eyes and long, lustrous black hair.

Lani was always glad to see Reid on any investigation. His seemingly unsinkable sense of corny humor and stream of dad jokes never failed to lift her spirits.

He shook her hand. "Good to see you, Lani," he said. "You know Sheree?"

"Of course. We worked on that case in Lanai, remember?"

Reid nodded. "Right, right. Good times. Well, except for the victim. Although I didn't hear him complain." White teeth flashed as he grinned.

Lani suppressed a groan.

Reid led Patel and Lani around his MPD van, out of sight of the media. He opened the sliding door and handed the women two bullet-resistant vests and helmets. "With a cop shooter on the premises, I thought it best not to take chances." He pulled his on, fastening the clips with practiced efficiency. "Be honest with me now. Does this vest make me look fat?"

"Handsome as ever, John," Lani said, laughing. "Come on." She led them across the back lawn to the path through the rain forest to the heiau.

As she stepped onto the forest floor, water dripped off leaves even though the rain had stopped hours earlier. Still, clouds appeared to be gathering again. Lani was glad, again, that she had chosen footwear suited to tromping through a rain forest. She had been surprised at the fashionable, but completely impractical footwear that FBI Agent Storm had worn. *She'll have to learn to adapt to Hawaii. Like the rest of us.*

But even though her hiking shoes were supposed to be waterproof, her feet were soon wet, as were the cuffs of her pants by the time they reached the remains of the koa tree that had been blown apart by the shot earlier.

Reid took a tape measure from his cargo pocket. "At a yard above the ground, this tree was a good ... eight inches in diameter," he said. Sheree Patel tapped on a tablet computer. "It took some serious caliber for one round to blow it apart like this, I'd say. Wooden you, Sheree?"

Reid's assistant rolled her eyes and continued to tap on her tablet.

"Now I know where to go when I want to get some wood," Lani joked, then immediately regretted it.

"Careful, Detective," Reid warned, grinning broadly. "That wasn't politically correct."

Patel rolled her eyes again. Lani took a deep breath and hoped she wasn't blushing. *That was worse than any of Reid's.*

"If it's a hefty round, it'll be easier to identify the gun it was fired from," she said. "Knowing it's a larger caliber firearm narrows down the possibilities."

"Good luck finding anything in this undergrowth," Reid said.

He started taking more measurements, like the distance from the koa to the heiau, the width of the path and the spacing between other trees.

Patel tapped to record every measurement, and in between took photos.

Reid looked down the path. "Can't really see the house or any other buildings from here. Which means it's pretty unlikely that whoever shot this tree to smithereens was shooting from there."

"Unless they weren't aiming for those three people in particular," Patel said.

The CSI investigators moved around, taking pictures and measurements. Lani looked at the sky, where the clouds kept getting lower and darker.

"Well, what do you know?" Sheree announced as Lani thought about getting back to shelter. Sheree was just off the path, close to the heiau, several yards away from the koa stump.

The small woman snapped on a pair of blue latex gloves, reached under a low, broad-leafed bush and held something up in triumph. "Does this look like a bullet? Big enough to kill an elephant." She dropped the object into a plastic bag and put a marker on the spot where the object had been.

"That's not a bullet. It's a shotgun slug. That's the only weapon that could have fired this monster," Reid said. He showed it to Lani.

In the bag was a blackened, distorted, shapeless hunk. "Deformed when it hit the tree trunk," she guessed.

"And deflected quite a lot, as well, unless I miss my guess," Reid answered. "That'll make it harder to determine which direction it was fired from.

"This is good work. Let's get back to shelter before the rain starts again."

They hustled down the path, toward the Sangster main house and its covered verandah and walkways.

Vanessa stepped into the Sangster household kitchen, which looked ready to serve a restaurant. The stainless steel counters were well-used. There was a gas stove with six burners, and a restaurant-style sink with a faucet that arched high over it. The refrigerator was big enough to house an airplane. Old-fashioned wooden chairs surrounded a large wooden table, and Vanessa wondered if the set had come from Sangster's parents' home in Texas.

Mai, the cook, stood behind the counter, her wide eyes staring at Vanessa. She held a knife that looked huge in her hand, a pile of chopped greens in front of her on the counter. "You want something to eat?" she said in her tiny voice.

"No, thank you, Mai. Can I call you Mai?"

The small woman nodded and resumed chopping vegetables.

"Tell me, how did you know Mr. Sangster?"

Without pausing her work, Mai replied, "I meet him in Oahu last year, after I arrive from Vietnam. He give me job as cook."

"Really? Just like that? Where did you meet

him? On the street?"

"No. I was working in restaurant in Honolulu. Clearing tables. Bussing."

"And he hired you as a cook."

Mai put down her knife and looked at the floor. "The restaurant fire me when he there. He feel sorry for me."

"So he made you a cook?"

"I train as chef in Vietnam. Come to America for work, but no one want me to be chef here. Mr. Sangster is ... was very kind to me." Tears ran down her cheeks.

"You're not legal here, are you, Mai?"

Mai turned to her, eyes wide in fear. She swallowed, but could say nothing.

"It's okay. Your secret is safe with me. But from now on, you tell me the truth about everything, all right?" Vanessa smiled at her. Mai nodded, wiped her face, and went back to chopping.

Paula Sangster, Jeffrey's wife, came into the kitchen at that point, her three young daughters trailing behind. "My girls did not get much of a breakfast before we had to leave Wailuku," she said to Mai, "and they haven't had lunch yet. Can we get something to eat? And maybe some coffee for me?"

"Yes, yes," Mai said. "I make."

Paula settled her girls around the kitchen table as Mai bustled around the cupboards and the enormous refrigerator, putting together a meal for young children with efficiency that impressed Vanessa.

The glass doors slid open. Vanessa turned to see a uniformed cop wearing a bulletproof vest and helmet step into the kitchen. "We found something that I think will interest you," he announced. He was tall and slim, with a white goatee. When he took off his helmet to wipe sweat off his forehead, he revealed thinning white hair. His blue eyes looked at her intensely.

"John Reid, Maui PD. I do most of the CSI here in Hana," he said, extending a hand.

Vanessa shook his hand. "Vanessa Storm, FBI."

Before the CSI investigator could say another word, Vanessa heard a knock behind her. She turned to see Josh Fong, the sound engineer, leaning into the kitchen. "Excuse me, Agent Storm? Would it be all right for me to go? I have some work to do."

"Where are you planning to go?" Vanessa asked.

"Just to the studio. There are some files I need to make sure don't get lost."

John Reid dropped a baggie onto the kitchen counter. Vanessa could not tell at first what was in it.

"Fine, Mr. Fong," she said, looking at the baggie. "As long as you do not leave the compound."

Vanessa turned her attention to the CSI head. It took a few seconds for her to figure out what she was looking at in the baggie. "A shotgun slug?"

"Well, it's not a snail so it must be a slug," Reid joked. His expression became serious again when he saw Vanessa's. "We found it on the ground beside that poor tree. I'm taking it to the lab, but it's from a shotgun, all right."

"Mr. Sangster have many guns," said Mai.

"That's right. He was known around here as a collector," Reid said.

"Thanks, Ms. Storm," said Fong, pushing past her and Reid to the deck. Vanessa registered it, storing the thought for later.

Lani Ferreira stepped into the kitchen, looking over her shoulder at Fong going along the covered wooden walkway. Her shoes and the cuffs of her pants were soaking wet. She pulled a smartphone out of her inner jacket pocket and looked at the screen. "I've got a text from the coroner. Early findings." She nodded toward the sliding doors. "Step out here with me for a minute."

Vanessa joined Lani on the large deck, sliding the door shut behind her. Below, a verdant lawn spread out, decorated with bright flower beds, to a series of outbuildings linked by a wooden walkway. "The coroner is saying the time of death was last night, probably before midnight, but the rain makes it impossible to pin that down. Also, Sangster's injuries are consistent with blunt force trauma to the head and body, and also consistent with a fall into the gully behind the heiau. And it appears he also had a heart attack."

"So did the heart attack cause the fall, or did the fall cause the heart attack?" Vanessa asked.

"He doesn't know yet. He's turning it over to the medical examiner for more study," Lani answered, tucking the phone back into a pocket. "It may take a couple of days, though."

"So you found the slug that blasted that poor tree apart. Any other evidence in the jungle?"

"The CSI team is trying to figure out where the slug was fired from," Lani answered. "When we found the slug, it was on the ground, not that close to the tree. It was probably deflected as it passed through the tree, but overall, we're guessing that it was fired from somewhere downhill—near the end of that house." She pointed to a separate building in the same style as the main house. A covered wooden walkway led to it from the rest of the compound. "The forest in almost every other direction has no line of sight."

"No one could see us, let alone shoot at us, unless they were at that building." Vanessa looked at the outbuildings, the garage that could house at least four cars. She knew from the FBI file that one of them was the studio—she guessed it was the one nearest the main house, the building that looked newest—and there were some guesthouses, or little apartments.

She looked up the mountain, but she could not see the heiau. Where could someone have stood to fire a shotgun at them, but not be seen by anyone at the house?

As she looked, big, heavy raindrops began falling, then faster and faster until they obscured the view.

"Where is Sangster's gun collection?" Vanessa asked, raising her voice over the rain.

"That's exactly what I was thinking," said Lani.

The two women went to look for Sangster's assistant, Isabel West. Before they got more than two steps away, strangers came around the corner of the wrap-around verandah.

First was a short, thin young Asian woman with long black hair, holding a microphone. Behind her came a tall, heavy man with a large video camera on his shoulder, and a smaller young man with a scruffy beard. A leather bag hung from a strap over his shoulder.

Behind them came a uniformed cop that Vanessa recognized from her last case in Hana, Officer Corinne O'Flynn, a young woman with brown hair, cut short. "You cannot come back here," she said to the TV news crew.

"Aisha Chen, KHIN Maui TV," said the thin woman. She strode forward and shoved her microphone under Vanessa's chin. "Is it true that foul play is suspected in the death of Steven Sangster?"

"No one has made any statement to that effect," said Vanessa.

"I already gave a statement to the press," Lani asserted, stepping between Vanessa and the reporter. "There is no new information at this time. Now get off the premises." She stepped forward, forcing Aisha Chen to step back.

"I'm sorry, Detective Ferreira," said Officer O'Flynn. "They got past me when I was looking the other way."

Vanessa told Officer O'Flynn to make sure the media stayed off the grounds, no closer than the entrance to the access road from the Hana Highway. Then she and Lani went to inspect Sangster's gun collection.

Isabel West used two keys and a combination on a keypad to unlock the steel door to a small, low building connected to the main house by the covered walkway. She led Lani, Vanessa and Officer Gilmour into a square room with the same wooden paneling and floors as the main house. Bars covered the two small windows. A sunshine ceiling let in the last of the day's light.

Sturdy-looking steel lockers lined one wall, padlocks on each one. Down the middle of the room stood a row of glass-topped display cases, holding at least twenty different guns.

"Mr. Sangster was an avid collector of firearms," Isabel said, looking a little embarrassed. "He especially liked antiques and curiosities. Those are in the glass display cases. The more modern ones are in the lockers."

"How many guns did he have?" Lani asked.

"I don't know, exactly," Isabel answered.

"Thirty-six," Officer Gilmour said. "Each has a trigger lock, the keys are stored securely, and the ammunition is stored separately, and locked up, too." When Lani and Vanessa stared at him, he added sheepishly, "I did an inspection last year, at his request. Mr. Sangster was a very responsible gun owner."

Vanessa walked along the display cases, admiring the collection. Sangster had appreciated the antiques, that was obvious. They sat on red velvet, each labelled. The guns seemed to be arranged chronologically, from two-hundred-year-old flintlocks to breechloaders, a Henry rifle from the Old West, an antique double-barreled shotgun with tooled breech, and at the end, a Luger automatic pistol and even an old model of her own sidearm. "A Walther PPK," said Lani.

"Not just for British spies," Vanessa retorted, smiling.

"Or Nazi dictators," Lani came back.

Vanessa turned to Isabel. "Do you notice anything missing, Ms. West?"

"No, but I never spend much time in here. Nothing seems to be missing from the display case, but I don't know about what's in the lockers."

"Who has the keys?" Lani asked.

"There is a set in Mr. Sangster's office. Plus, Kaholo Iolani has a full set, too."

"The groundskeeper? Why?"

"They went hunting together. Well, they used to, they tell me. I've never known Mr. Sangster to go hunting since I've been working here."

"Is there an inventory?" Vanessa said.

"In the office, on Mr. Sangster's computer."

"Give the keys to Officer Gilmour. Officer, get a CSI team in here and make sure every item on that inventory is accounted for."

They left Sangster's personal armory, Isabel locking the door again.

"Given the number of people involved, I think we should split up the interviews between us," Vanessa said to Lani. "We can meet this evening and compare notes."

"Sure," said Lani. "If you talk with the kids, I'll start with the widow."

"Which one?"

"I hear you. Let's start with the current one."

"I kind of wanted to talk to Erica Harrison," Vanessa said.

Lani smiled, looking up from under her eyebrows. "Sorry. I'm an even bigger fan of hers than you were of Steven Sangster's."

Lani left to find Kathryn Sangster and Erica Harrison. Vanessa went to the dead man's study, taking the opportunity to check her voicemail as she walked. The message was from the last voice she wanted to hear at that moment. She groaned. "Hey, baby, it's me. Surprise! I just landed in Honolulu."

Perry Boyd. How did he get this number? From my parents, of course. He always could charm them.

They're not the only ones. A painful image threatened to rise in her mind, and she quickly thought about work, a technique she had learned over the years.

She had no time for Perry Boyd now. She turned off the phone and went to look for the enigmatic Sophia Keahi.

Chapter 4:
The singer's wives

With Vanessa Storm in Sangster's office, Lani set up in the dining room. She had left her wet running shoes near the kitchen door, and removed her socks, too. Her pants were drying, but still damp, so she sat carefully, hoping not to get too much water on the fine upholstery of the dining room chair.

As she had said to FBI Agent Storm, she planned to talk to the current widow first, saving the best, Erica Harrison, for last.

Kathryn's high heels clacked on the wood floor and her brassy hair bounced over her shoulders as she walked in.

"I'm very sorry for your loss, Mrs. Sangster," Lani said.

"Everybody's 'sorry,'" Kathryn replied, sitting across the broad cherrywood table from Lani. "What do you want? I have arrangements to make."

"Yes, I'm sure. I won't take much of your time. For accuracy, I'm recording this conversation." Lani indicated her smartphone on the table, with the Record app open. Kathryn nodded. "When was the last time you saw your husband?"

"Yesterday, in the evening."

"He didn't come to bed with you? Did that not concern you at the time?"

"Not really. He's been stayin' up late a lot, lately, playing his guitar and supposedly workin' on new songs."

"Supposedly?"

Kathryn shrugged and picked at a thread on the seam of her jeans. "He didn't seem to be makin' much progress. Not that I heard, anyway. But he and Josh would stay up till all hours in his studio."

"Josh Fong, the sound engineer."

"Yah, that's him."

"You don't seem to like him very much."

Kathryn shrugged again, looking at something interesting outside the window. Lani looked, too, but saw only the dark grey rain. "He's all right," Kathryn said at last. "But I never had much to do with him, y'understand? He was always workin' with Steve. And with Isabel."

"How do you feel about Ms. Harrison coming here? Another of your husband's wives in your home?"

Kathryn's eyes flashed momentarily, but then she looked away, toward a gold record hanging on the wall. It was a duet with Sangster and Harrison, "We're Starting All Over," which had gone to number one on the country charts. "It's fine. I've always been a fan of Erica Harrison. I was hoping to maybe work with her, too."

"You're a singer, yourself, aren't you, Mrs. Sangster?" Lani asked.

She smiled a little. "All my life. Steve just finished writin' a bunch of songs for me to sing, and we'd started recordin' 'em. He said he knew they would do real well. That I had the perfect voice for New Country. Steve told me he'd join in singin' on some, and I was hopin' maybe to sing with him on his next ..." Her voice caught and Vanessa could see a tear in her eye. She wiped it with the back of her hand. "I'm sorry. It comes over me in waves." She took a deep breath and another tear spilled over her cheek, smearing her makeup.

"That's all right, Mrs. Sangster. I understand."

She stood and went to the window, leaning on the sill and staring into the darkness. The wind drove the rain against the window, making rivers on the glass.

"He told me, before we were married, that I have a unique voice, a special talent." She took a deep, shaking breath.

Lani gave her a minute before asking one more question. "So, last night, before you went to bed, the last time you saw your husband, he was in the studio with Mr. Fong?" Lani knew that Kathryn had already said she had last seen Steven in the afternoon, but the idea was to ask for the same information in different ways to uncover lies.

"Yes, that's right," Kathryn answered, her voice clear. "That was the last time I saw him alive." Lani detected an angry note in her tone.

"And when did you learn he was dead?"

Kathryn swallowed before continuing. "This mornin', when Kaholo ran into the house, yellin' that Steve was dead up at the old native ruin."

"The heiau?"

"Yeah, that's what they call it. Well, that brought a big commotion. Everybody ran up the path, but Kaholo wouldn't let anybody near him. He kept yellin' not to touch him, let the police come and do their job. He wouldn't even let me near him. My own husband." Her voice was steady, calm, as she stared into the darkness.

Lani decided to direct the conversation away from the death scene. "Yesterday, were you home all day, Mrs. Sangster? Did you have dinner with Mr. Sangster?"

Kathryn turned toward her, a puzzled expression on her face. "No, I did not. I had dinner at a restaurant in Hana with a couple of girlfriends."

"What time did you get home?"

"Probably around ten."

"Did you notice anything unusual?"

Kathryn frowned, worry beginning to creep into her expression. "No, nothing ... well, come to think of it, a car came out of the access road to the estate just before I turned into it. I had to wait on the highway to let it out, actually. I didn't think much of it at the time, but the only cars that would come down that road would come from the estate."

"So, it would have to have been someone who was here?"

"Yes."

"And that didn't concern you?"

"I didn't really think about it. It was probably someone comin' to do somethin' at the studio for Steve. He was makin' some improvements, addin' all kinds of high-tech electronic stuff."

"So, he was in the studio all day and all evening, as far as you know?"

"That's what I thought."

"And when did he go up to the heiau?"

Kathryn shrugged again. "I do not know. I just don't know."

Lani changed direction. "Do you have the keys to your late husband's gun collection?"

"No. That was Steve's thing. Him and Kaholo loved those old guns."

"Do you know how to use a gun?" Lani asked, careful to keep her tone even. She felt her pulse throb on the side of her head. *That's not good.*

I really hate getting shot at. But I guess everybody does.

"Of course. I'm from Kentucky. My daddy taught me how to use a gun and a rifle. How to look after them, too. But I never felt I needed that kinda protection here in Hawaii."

If you only knew how dangerous people can be, even in Hawaii, Lani thought. "Thank you, Mrs. Sangster. That's all the questions I have for now.

Please, don't let me keep you any longer."

"This *is* my dinin' room, you know. I'm lettin' you use it."

"I appreciate that, Mrs. Sangster. And with your permission, I'll just need to use it a little longer." She walked Kathryn to the double French doors that separated it from the living room, shook her hand and said, "If there is anything I can do …"

Kathryn shook her head a little and walked away, her heels clacking on the hardwood floor. Lani watched her, wondering why she was certain the lady was lying.

She found Erica Harrison upstairs, unpacking a single suitcase in one of the many guest bedrooms. For a moment, Lani was a starstruck teenager. Seeing the singer brought back memories of Erica Harrison on a TV program, singing a duet with her then-husband, Steven Sangster, the handsomest man in country music.

Even today, close to twenty years later, Erica Harrison retained her shape and her audience. Grey edged her signature long black tresses and crow's feet bracketed her big, dark eyes. But she was still beautiful, and Lani felt again that old pang, that self-consciousness about her untameable curls. "How are you, Ms. Harrison?" she asked.

"Please, call me Erica," she said, sitting on the edge of the bed. She took a packet of cigarettes from her purse, offered one to Lani, shrugged when she refused and lit one. After a comforting drag, she said, "It was such a shock. I told you, I was on my way over here. I tuned in a local radio station, and it announced that Steven was dead. I had to pull over to the side of the road." She held up a hand. "I think I just now stopped shaking over it."

Lani sat on an upholstered chair. "So you say that Steven invited you down here?"

"Weeks ago. I hadn't heard a word from him in years, then suddenly he emailed me a link to digital samples of new songs he had written. They were surprisingly good."

"Surprisingly?"

Erica smiled apologetically. "It's no secret that Steven's career went downhill more than ten years ago. He hasn't had a successful new recording in a long time. In my opinion—which I shared with him, more than once—he was trying too hard to fit into the 'New Country' style. He turned away from the music that made him Steven Sangster."

"The folksy stuff."

Erica shrugged. "You could call it that. But Steven's sound was unique to Steven."

Lani had to agree with that. "When was the last time you spoke with Mr. Sangster?"

"Two years ago?" Erica said, shaking her head. "We exchanged electronic messages more than spoke, recently. Steven really got into technology in the past few years. He invited me by email, sent song samples by file transfer. I agreed to come the same way."

Lani changed direction. "You seem to get along with his daughter."

"I always got along with Steven's and Frances's kids as children."

"Jeffrey, too?"

Erica looked away. "Not as much, lately. Jeff became a financial manager and convinced Steven to let him look after his investments. I think, and I'm not alone in this, that he's been more interested in preserving his own inheritance than in protecting his father's interests."

"Wouldn't those be the same?"

"Not always. Jeff actually prevented Steven from getting enough money to promote his last album. He said it would be a flop, like the one before it, and it was a self-fulfilling prophecy without any promotion."

That was interesting, Lani thought, but did not shed much light on the case. "Does he have enemies?"

Erica shook her head, a strange little smile twisting her mouth. "Probably. He's not the most likeable guy. But I don't know whether he's pissed anyone off enough to try to kill him."

There was nothing else to ask this woman who had arrived after all the action. "Thank you, Ms. Harrison—Erica, I mean. If you think of anything else that might help this investigation, please don't hesitate to tell me, or any of the other police officers."

"Of course," she said.

As she returned to the dining room, she spotted Janet Sangster and her boyfriend in the living room. Lani decided to do Vanessa a favor. "Janet, can I speak with you?" she asked and stepped into the dining room.

Janet froze, hand at her throat. She hesitantly followed Lani into the dining room, glancing over her shoulder.

Lani gestured toward a chair. "I'd like to speak to you and Kefir, I mean, 'Keefer,' as well. Please, sit down." Lani said.

As Lani closed the door, Janet sat at the table, Kefir slouching behind her. He did not look at Lani, but only at the floor or the table. "Thank you," said Lani when they were all seated. She pointed to her smartphone, set to Record again. "I just want to ask you a few questions. I understand how this may be somewhat painful, but it's important. Janet, when did you last see your father?"

"You mean, before … ?" Lani nodded. "Yesterday," she said in a small voice, glancing over at Kefir momentarily.

"What time was that?"

"About, oh, nine o'clock or so. Nine at night."

"Where?"

Again, Janet looked at her boyfriend, who looked back and then at Lani with challenge in his eyes.

"He was going into his studio," Janet said

finally.

"By himself?"

"No, he was with ... with Josh Fong and ..." her voice trailed off.

"Yes? With Josh Fong and who else?"

Janet looked at Lani with an open mouth, then at her boyfriend. Kefir finally spoke up. "Me. I was there."

"You? What were you doing, Mr. Steinberg?"

"We were sharing a joint, okay?" he snarled, leaning over the table.

"Kefir ..." Janet warned, but he waved her off.

"Yeah, Steve liked his weed. And he liked to share it, too. So him, me and Josh had a toke before he went to play some songs. It helped him come up with ideas. Okay? You gonna arrest me for that?"

"Kefir," Janet moaned again.

"Do I have to arrest you, Kefir?" Lani asked. "You already have a long rap sheet. Tell me, do you own a firearm?"

Kefir stood, cocked a hip and held his arms out to the sides, a weird combination of defiant cockiness and submission. "You wanna frisk me? Get a thrill?"

"How about you just cooperate with this investigation. I'd think you owe Steven Sangster that much." Lani knew that last statement was way over the line, but she could not keep it in.

"I owe, I owe, yadda-yadda-yadda," Kefir said. "I don't need this. I'll cooperate if you ask me questions, Mrs. Lady Cop, but I don't need this right now." He strode out of the room.

Janet stared after him, open-mouthed. She turned to Lani. "I'm sorry," she began as tears spilled down her cheeks.

"It's okay," Lani said. "I'll talk to him soon enough. I know this is hard, Janet. I have lost a parent, too." Lani forced herself not to feel the whirlwind of conflicting emotions she associated with her father's death. "But just tell me how your father seemed last evening."

"He was in a good mood," Janet said. She sat back in the chair and sighed. "Of course, that was probably the weed talking. But he wasn't depressed or anything. He seemed really excited lately about the new songs he was recording."

"For Kathryn?"

Janet waved her hand. "Not really. He said those were, oh what was the word? 'Formulaic.' Kathryn likes the 'New Country' stuff. Not like my dad's music at all. But Dad was excited about this new project. He thought the songs he was going to record with Erica were really good. He said they were like his old stuff, but different. Anyway, that's what he said."

"Why would he walk out to the heiau at night?"

Janet looked out the window at the rain. "He loved that old thing. I don't know why—it's just a pile of old rocks to me. But he said it inspired him. And he was going to leave it to the Hawaiians."

"The Hawaiians?"

"Well, some group that looks after old historical things," said Janet.

"He told you this?"

"Sure. He told everybody." She leaned closer and whispered to Lani, "But he didn't tell everybody this part. He was leaving the ruins to the Hawaiians, but the house and the rest of the estate to me."

"Really? Have you seen his will?"

Janet leaned back again, pouting a little. "Well, no. But Dad wouldn't lie to me about something like that."

Lani thought about that for a minute. "All right. Thanks very much for your help, Janet."

Chapter 5:
The road to Hana

Vanessa found Sophia Keahi sitting at the kitchen table with Mai, the cook. Steaming cups of tea sat in front of both of them. Sophia looked up at Vanessa with a gentle smile.

Vanessa sat across from the older woman. "Tell me, Ms. Keahi, how you heard about Mr. Sangster?"

"He was a good friend," Sophia repeated. "Of course, I came as soon as I knew he had passed."

"You did not answer my question."

"I call her," Mai said, her voice tiny.

Sophia patted the young woman's hand. "Mai is a good friend, too. She has been since she arrived."

"I see. All right, then, when did you arrive? Today at the Sangster home, I mean?"

Sophia paused, looking deeply into Vanessa's eyes long enough to make Vanessa want to squirm. But she did not show it. "I came as soon as I heard. I suppose I arrived ... perhaps about half past nine." Mai nodded agreement.

"All right. And where were you yesterday evening? We need to know this to rule out ...

possibilities." Vanessa's own apologetic tone surprised her.

Sophia smiled again. "In the evening, I was at a prayer meeting at the cultural center until past nine. Then I went home, read a little while and went to bed."

"Can anyone corroborate that?"

"The Hana Cultural Club, for the prayer meeting. After that, since I live alone, you will have to take my word for it."

"Makuahine Sophie never tell a lie," Mai said.

She called her "auntie." Vanessa's next words again surprised her.

"That's all right. I never doubted you." She stood. "That is all. Ms. Keahi, I will have to ask you to leave the estate now, and not to talk to anyone else in the household until our initial investigation is complete."

Sophia nodded, still smiling her little smile. Vanessa left for Steven Sangster's office. On the way there, Isabel West, the personal assistant, came running around the corner and nearly crashed into her. Vanessa barely had a moment to blurt out "Don't leave the estate," before the young woman ran out to the covered walkway that linked the main house to the outbuildings.

Vanessa took the swivel chair behind Steven Sangster's desk, conscious that she was taking the place of the famous singer. The office was a very different place from the rest of the house, appointed in a Western style. The desk, table, credenza and shelves were made of inlaid wood in five-pointed star patterns. Scattered woven rugs covered part of the hardwood floor. A couch was upholstered in a pattern of beige, gold and black, rather than the floral design that seemed mandated in Hawaii.

Gold records covered one wall, and a stuffed leather couch dominated the wall between two windows that looked toward the nearly dark ocean. Jeffrey Sangster perched at the end of the couch far from Vanessa, his eyes roving around the room, looking everywhere but at her.

She took out her tablet computer for note-taking. "You live in Wailuku, correct?" It was an expensive area of modern houses with manicured lawns.

"Yes. That's why it took so long to get here. The Hana Highway gets more and more traffic, the later in the day it gets."

"You're a stockbroker, is that correct?"

"Investment adviser. Look, what does this have to do with my father's...my father's death?"

"I'm just checking on the accuracy of our file, Mr. Sangster. Now, when did you arrive—"

"Hold it. The FBI has a file on me? Why?"

"We do not have a file on you, Mr. Sangster. We have had a file on your father for some time, but not much more than you'd find on Wikipedia. He was prominent, travelled outside the country frequently and did officially represent the United States at some functions in the past."

"I see."

"When did you say you arrived in Hana, Mr. Sangster?"

"Just today. We left as soon as we heard," he answered, too quickly.

"What time today?"

"We only heard about the...about my father around 9 a.m. I was already at work, and the girls were in school by then. By the time Paula—my wife—called me, then I got home, then we had to pick up the girls, and of course they had to have some lunch, and then there was traffic...well, we didn't get here till close to four in the afternoon."

To Vanessa, the explanation had too many details, as if Jeffrey had been thinking of it and rehearsing it in his mind. She watched Jeffrey pick up a pen that happened to be on the end table beside the couch, take off the cap and put it on again. He turned to look out the window, and dissatisfied with the darkness, stood and looked closely at one of the gold records on the wall. "I never liked this song," he said. "One of his biggest sellers. I never understood the appeal."

Vanessa went to stand beside Jeffrey. "There's Something in a Sunday." Vanessa had always loved that song. She remembered sitting in her bedroom, playing it over and over again on her portable stereo, hitting the Back button so she could hear it again. When she was eleven, that song seemed to have more meaning than anything else in the world. She felt a tear well up in one eye. "That was the one that he said allowed him to quit working for a living," she said.

"Never understood the appeal," Jeffrey repeated.

Vanessa swallowed what felt like a brick. "Were you close with your father? Lately, I mean?"

Jeffrey turned quickly and stepped back, staring with wide eyes at Vanessa. "Close? Sure," he sputtered. "We were father and son. We visited each other. I talked with him by phone a couple of times a week, and I managed his investments. Kept him solvent."

"Did you have major disagreements?"

"Well, everyone has some disagreements. Nothing out of the ordinary." Sangster returned to the couch and sat down, crossing his legs and looking out the dark window again.

"You said earlier that recording another album was an unnecessary risk. Why do you say that?"

"Because he's spending a fortune on new electronic sound equipment, upgrading the studio, and paying that engineer, Josh Fong, a ridiculous amount. He even put him up in one of the guest apartments on the estate."

"But he's making a new album."

"Another flop, you mean. It'll cost more than it will ever make. He hasn't had a hit in years. He hasn't even played on stage in ten. Music has changed in the past twenty years. People don't want the same things they did when Steve Sangster was topping the charts."

It's too bad. "You also characterized your father as 'stubborn,'" Vanessa said.

"Well, he was stubborn. Everybody knows that. He insisted that his new album would make millions. He refused to take my advice. But that doesn't mean we didn't love each other."

Vanessa looked at him closely. A vein throbbed in his forehead. She didn't say anything, just watched him look at the empty window. She heard the sound of returning rain on the glass. After a minute of silence, Jeffrey turned to her again. "What am I being accused of?"

"Nothing, Mr. Sangster. No one is accusing anyone of anything."

"He promised to leave the house and the grounds to me in his will, but if his estate carries a ton of debt from useless advertising, the value won't mean a thing. He also told me that he wanted me to administer his estate after he ... after he passed."

That's a strange thing to bring up now.

"Do you have any enemies, Mr. Sangster?"

"What do you mean?"

"Is there anyone you can think of who has a reason to try to shoot you?"

Sangster swallowed as sweat appeared on his

high forehead. "I ... uh, no ... no one I can think of."

Vanessa just looked at him for a long time. *He is lying, but not about anything I've asked him. There's something he's hiding, something he's hoping I won't ask about.*

"Thank you, that's all. Can you send in Mrs. Sangster, please? Your wife, I mean."

Jeffrey stood up quickly, looked as if he was going to say something, then turned quickly and left the room.

Isabel West, Sangster's personal assistant, appeared in the doorway. She checked the corridor both ways, stepped into the study and shut the door behind her. Then she stood there, looking alternately at the floor and at Vanessa, rubbing one hand up and down her other forearm.

"What's wrong, Ms. West?" Vanessa asked.

She looked up at Vanessa, one hand resting on the other forearm. Her eyebrows seemed to be trying to hug each other for comfort. "Steve's ... Mr. Sangster's new music is gone," she whispered hoarsely.

Paula Sangster opened the door and glared at Isabel. "I thought you wanted to speak to me next," she snapped.

"Just one moment please, Mrs. Sangster," Vanessa said, letting Isabel into the office and closing the door before Paula could say anything more.

In the office, Isabel paced the wooden floor, continuing to rub her forearm. "I've checked all the drives, all the servers, the computer in his studio and the laptop in his bedroom. They're not there, and he always kept backups. I even checked his iPad and the cloud account." She came around the desk to the computer. "May I?"

Vanessa nodded as Isabel moved the mouse and clicked on the keyboard. Vanessa watched her open window after window, shaking her head in disappointment every time.

"Do you mean the songs he wrote for Kathryn?" Vanessa asked.

Isabel gave a dismissive little laugh. "No, unfortunately. No, the missing ones are *good*. As good as his old stuff. The songs he wrote for Kathryn don't even sound like Steven Sangster wrote them. He's trying to please her by writing 'New Country' songs." She made little air quotes with her fingers. "He told me he doesn't even like her singing voice.

"The songs I'm looking for were the ones he wanted for his own next album," Isabel continued. "That was why he invited Erica Harrison down here. He wanted her to help him finish them and record them together with him. They were great, and now they're gone."

"Could it be some kind of computer glitch?"

Isabel shook her head. "Not with that many backups at once. That's no coincidence. Someone erased them."

Isabel stood, making a gesture toward the

computer that looked like defeat. Vanessa indicated one of the sofas in the office, and sat in the guest chair in front of the desk.

Isabel sat on the couch, perching like the younger Sangster had before. Her hand resumed rubbing her forearm. "All his new songs, gone. He called them his legacy."

"If these are the songs he wrote for Erica Harrison, she should have digital copies. She said he'd sent them to her."

"Those were just parts of early drafts. Not even whole songs. Since he sent them, he's done a lot of work. The files had later versions with fuller sound, notes, different lyrics and different ideas. No, the songs are gone." Isabel dropped her head into her hands. "Someone erased them. Stole them."

"When was the last time you saw the files?"

Isabel bit her bottom lip and looked at nothing as she thought. "Yesterday. I saw them on the computer monitor in the studio."

"You said you saw them in the studio. Was he there with Mr. Fong?" Isabel nodded. "Is there any reason Mr. Fong would delete the files?"

Isabel looked at Vanessa with wide eyes. "I can't imagine."

"Thank you for telling me. I'll keep it in mind as a factor in the investigation. In the meantime, Ms. West, please don't search anymore through Mr. Sangster's effects until the investigation is over. All right?" Isabel nodded, eyes wide. She still rubbed her forearm.

"While you're here, can I ask you a few questions?" Vanessa reached behind her for the file on Sangster's desk. "When did you last see Steven Sangster?"

Isabel swallowed and looked down at the floor again. "Yesterday, late afternoon. Here in this study. We talked about the arrangements for Ms. Harrison, his second wife, to come here. I checked on her flight reservations, then I went to make sure her guest room was ready. Steve told me he was going to the studio with Josh."

"How long have you worked for Mr. Sangster?"

"Almost two years, now. Two years in July."

"And what is the nature of your work? 'Personal assistant' is a little vague."

"I help manage his different affairs—some financial transactions, organizing his calendar, dealing with media inquiries, some correspondence. I manage things like arranging for Josh Fong to come here when Steve wants ... wanted to record ..." Her voice faltered and she choked. A tear spilled over her cheek. "I'm sorry. It's just such a shock ..."

Vanessa gave her a moment, then asked, "How did you come to start working for Mr. Sangster?"

Isabel swallowed, looking up at one of the gold records. "It's incredible to me how many hits he had, one after the other, and then, nothing. It's like the audience broke up with him. That's how I started working for him. I fell in love with his music when I was a teenager. I don't know why, but somehow it spoke to me. It reached a part of me like nothing else ever had." She looked directly at Vanessa, half her mouth smiling. "I used to dream about being a musician, about performing on stage with Steve Sangster, the 'Texan silver-tongued devil.' Then I realized I had no musical talent, at all. But I learned in college that I *did* have a talent for business management. I read in one of the gossip websites that Steve was talking about a comeback, about making a new album. I scraped together all my savings, flew to Maui, showed up at his door and asked for the job."

"And he hired you? Just like that?"

Isabel laughed a little, looking away from Vanessa again. "I guess I was lucky that Mrs. Sangster—Kathryn, I mean, the current Mrs. Sangster—was out of town that week. Visiting her mother, I think. Steve has a soft spot for young people looking for work. When I told him I had nowhere else to go and no money left to get anywhere, I guess he felt sorry for me. He let me stay in one of the guest apartments, for a few days at first. Then he started asking me to do a few organizational things for him, then more and more. And now, well, here I am. Happy to be working for the great American songwriter as he creates his last ..." She choked again and more tears rolled down her face.

Vanessa went to sit beside her. She put a hand

on Isabel's shoulder and said, "I'm very sorry, Ms. West. I won't bother you any longer, except for one last question."

Isabel nodded, biting her bottom lip and looking at the floor. "Were you in love with Steve Sangster?"

Isabel gasped, looking up at Vanessa with wide eyes and open mouth. "What? What are you saying?"

"Were you in love with him?"

Isabel's mouth opened and closed. She rubbed her arm and looked all around the study as if the answer were hidden somewhere. "I respected him. I loved his music, I still do, I love him ... *loved* him as a friend, as a Christian is required to love her neighbor ..." She stood, walked to the door, turned and walked to the window, turned again and seemed to be lost in the room. "Mr. Sangster is a married man, Ms. Storm. *Was* a married man."

Vanessa nodded, careful to keep any expression off her face. "Thank you, Ms. West. That's all I have for now."

"Wait," Isabel said. "There is something I have to show you." She went behind the desk, opened a file drawer and pulled out a sheet of paper. *She knew exactly where it was,* Vanessa noticed.

Isabel handed her the sheet. "Steven wrote this letter a year ago. He told me that, if anything happened to him, he wanted *me* to take over administration of his finances from Jeff."

Vanessa read the letter. In official language, it confirmed what the assistant told her. "What prompted him to worry about something happening to him, Ms. West?"

"Steven had a health scare last year. It turned out to be minor, but for a little while, we thought he was having a heart attack." She leaned closer to Vanessa. "He also told me to get rid of Josh Fong and replace him with a different sound engineer."

"Thank you, Ms. West." Vanessa handed the letter back to her. "Please put this back where you found it, and please don't disturb any more of Mr. Sangster's things by looking for those files, all right?"

Isabel stared at her for a long minute. Finally, she took a deep breath, nodded and left.

Paula Sangster came in then, radiating anger. "It's getting late. My kids have not eaten supper yet, and I had to wait for...for *her*?" Vanessa decided that the trace of an accent was Spanish.

"Please sit down, Mrs. Sangster." Vanessa held a hand toward the sofa, but Paula leaned against the desk, instead, her arms crossed in front of her. Vanessa took a moment to look at her carefully. Long hair streaked in multiple shades of brown, a long, tanned face, long, fake nails. Her large eyes were brown, her lips full. She was almost beautiful, Vanessa thought, but something was off. Maybe it was the anger coming from every pore. She wore a stylish blouse over skinny jeans that were just a little too tight for her wide hips, and the highest heels that Vanessa had ever seen—which meant that she was considerably shorter without them.

"First, I'm very sorry for your loss, Mrs. Sangster," Vanessa began.

She made a dismissive gesture. "He wasn't my father; he was my husband's. I'm here for him."

What a reaction to have. "May I call you Paula? There are so many 'Mrs. Sangsters' here today."

"Of course," she answered, and surprised Vanessa with a smile.

"Did you dislike Steven Sangster, Paula?"

The smile disappeared as Paula drew her head back, a gesture of confusion. "No, no, of course not. I just meant that it affects my husband much more than me. And my daughters. He was their *tito.*"

That decides it; it's a Spanish accent.

"He really loved them. He always said that he would provide for them after he was gone. I liked Steven. He did take up a lot of my husband's time, though."

"How so?"

"Jeff manages his investment accounts. He doesn't make any money from it, and Steven always argues...argued against Jeff's advice."

"What kind of advice?"

"Oh, I don't know—investments, stocks, expenses, things like that. It's not my business, so I don't bother with the details. But I know that Jeff is always worrying about his father's accounts. He spends more time managing his father's funds than all the rest of his clients combined."

Vanessa settled into an easy chair and looked up at Paula. "You seem to have some resentment toward Isabel West."

Paula's eyes flashed and Vanessa saw two spots flush on her cheeks under her tan. "Not at all," she said, her nostrils flaring.

"No? Do you think she was giving Mr. Sangster good service?"

Paula's eyes widened. "Oh, she was giving him—" She stopped herself and took a deep breath. "I would not know. She has not been here very long."

Vanessa looked at Paula intensely for a long moment, until Paula stood up and walked over to look at one of the gold records. "'There's something in a Sunday,'" she said. "That was always my favorite Steven Sangster song."

The same one that her husband said he didn't like.

"When did you hear about Steven's death?"

Paula looked up, thinking. "Isabel telephoned around nine in the morning. I had just come home from dropping the girls at school. They go to a private school in Wailuku."

"What was your reaction when you heard?"

"I was shocked, of course. Steven wasn't that old, and he seemed to be in good health."

"What did you do?"

"I called Jeff at work, of course. He came home

right away, and then we got the girls from school, and we drove to Hana. It's a slow drive."

"Yes, I know. I drove it myself today." She stood, rising over Paula's head despite the latter's high heels. "Thank you. That's all the questions I have for now."

Paula looked surprised. "Oh. Okay." She turned and left, pausing at the door to look one more time at Vanessa, then left.

Vanessa typed out a few notes on her tablet, tucked it into her shoulder bag, and went looking for Kaholo Iolani.

A side door opened onto a covered walkway linking the houses. She could barely see the ground below with the rain pelting down. As she passed the corner of the main house, the onshore wind drove cold raindrops under the roof, splattering her side and legs. She held her shoulder bag against her body and ran to the next building, regretting again that she was wearing her Vince Camuto shoes.

The door to the next building was open, spilling light onto the walkway. The awning over it was wide enough to keep the rain out. Vanessa stepped inside quickly, grateful to be out of the wind and wet.

Warm, yellowish light illuminated wood-paneled walls, a braided rug in the middle of the teak floor, microphone stands like disorganized sentries and three guitars on their own stands in front of a drum set. One wall was a window in front of a sound mixing panel, covered with dozens of sliding knobs, and behind that, six different, tall speakers.

On an office swivel chair sat a thin Asian man in a dark blue hoodie. His eyebrows rose when Vanessa stepped in. He stood, taking off the headphones he was wearing and came out of the control booth. "Agent Storm," said Josh Fong. "Can I help you?"

"I'd like to ask you a few questions."

"Sure," he said and sat on a high chair. Vanessa suddenly pictured the lanky Steven Sangster sitting on it, one foot hooked onto the crossbar, the other long leg stretched out to the floor, a twelve-string acoustic guitar in front of his chest.

Fong was shorter and thinner than Sangster had been, though, and his eyes were dark brown, not blue. Vanessa put down her shoulder bag on the leather sofa, but remained standing. "First, how long have you worked for Mr. Sangster?"

"Not long. I worked for a studio in California a couple of years ago, and did some remixing of some of his old songs. He liked what I did, and a couple of months ago, he sent me an email asking me to come out here and record some new songs."

"And when did you get to Hana?"

"About four weeks ago. Steve wanted me to get things set up and to try out some new material before Erica Harrison came to do some duets. He was really working hard on those songs. He said he didn't care if he sold a single copy, as long as they would be the best songs he could record."

Four weeks ago. Which means that Isabel West was lying when she said that Steven Sangster wanted to replace him a year ago. Unless he said that recently.

It seemed Steven Sangster had said different things to everyone. "It was going to be just the two of them? No band, no backup singers?"

Fong shrugged. "At first, anyway. He did say something about maybe bringing in some other musicians, depending on how things went. And also, Kathryn has been laying down some tracks, too. Steve wrote a bunch for her. In the 'New Country' style."

"Kathryn Sangster—the widow?" Vanessa played it ignorant. "She's a singer, too?"

Fong shrugged again. "She wants to be. Her voice requires some ..." he waved one hand back and forth as he searched for the word. "... production. And she'll need a band behind her if she ever wants to release anything. Steve said he believed in her, though.

"Do you want to hear one of her songs?"

Vanessa shrugged. "Sure.""

Fong went to a laptop computer and tapped. He flipped some switches on the sound board, and the studio filled with the sound of Steven Sangster's guitar. A sound that made Vanessa want to weep.

Then came the vocals.

"That's Kathryn?" Vanessa asked. Josh nodded. "Well ... there are a lot of country singers with voices that ... aren't *technically* great."

"You could say that."

Vanessa endured the song for another thirty seconds. "Okay, I think I have an idea now."

Fong turned off the playback. "Now you know what I have to work with."

That was awful. But there are more important things I need to understand. "Where have you been staying these past four weeks?" she asked Fong.

"At first, I was in the big hotel in Hana, what's it called...weird name...oh, yah, the Travaasa. But Steve likes—I mean, liked to work late into the night." Fong looked down at his lap, picking at a loose thread on the seam of his chinos. "So eventually, uh, Kathryn told Steve to let me stay in one of the guest apartments."

"Just how many guest apartments does this place have?"

Fong shrugged yet again, looking at something very interesting on his shoe. "I dunno. There's some guest rooms in the main house and some other units in the other buildings."

Vanessa studied his profile for a long moment, the way the black hair hung down over one side of his face, the thin, untidy facial hair that indicated he wanted to grow a beard but really couldn't. He had wide shoulders and tough-looking hands, though, that contrasted with his baby face. "So, you've been here for two weeks, working with the late Steve Sangster on his new material, and that's all you've been doing? Doesn't it get kind of boring?"

Fong looked at the ceiling. "Well, there is actually a lot to keep you occupied in Hana. This is a tropical paradise, right? There's always something to do. Working on Steve's music is pretty time-consuming, anyway."

"Do you work out, Mr. Fong?"

This time, he looked at her. "Sure, all the time. Well, I used to—there's no gym here at the estate. I've done some hiking on the trails here with Kathryn." He stopped speaking suddenly, pupils dilated. "Steve didn't like to go hiking. He said his knees were too sore."

Vanessa nodded, studying Fong quietly. After a pause she said, "Now that Mr. Sangster is dead, what are your plans?"

"I guess I'll go back to the mainland and my old job."

"Which was?"

"Sound engineer."

"Where?"

"Different studios in L.A. Whoever wants to work with me. I'm getting pretty well-known in the L.A. scene, so there's always plenty of work. Pretty soon, I should be a music producer." His chest puffed out a little, and his chin rose.

"That's good. But don't leave before the Sheriff's Department says they've concluded their investigation, or at least, concluded their interest in you."

Fong's eyes grew wide. "Am I a suspect?"

Vanessa tilted her head and looked directly into Fong's eyes. "Why would you say that, Mr. Fong? No one is a suspect, yet. We do not yet have a definitive homicide."

"What about the gunshot?"

Vanessa watched his face as she thought about her answer. "We will eliminate the possibilities until we have determined who made that shot."

Fong swallowed. "You said I can't go back home."

"If Mr. Sangster died of natural causes, the investigation will close quickly. Which means you should have no problems with returning to California, or going anywhere else, for that matter. But I doubt very much that anyone is going anywhere off the island today," she said with a nod toward the window and the pelting rain.

Fong swallowed again. "Oh, yah. Right. Okay." He stood up from the chair and moved back toward the control booth. "Umm, d'you mind? I was working on something when you came in."

"Would you know what happened to the new songs Steven Sangster was working on?"

He looked up quickly, eyebrows drawing together. "Yah, Isabel told me about that. Came in here a little while ago, frantic, searching all the computer drives and servers. I dunno what happened. Steven must have moved 'em sometime last night, after I went to bed. He was always workin' late." He spoke very quickly, and Vanessa thought she detected a trace of an accent. "But what does it matter now, anyway? Steven died without finishing his songs. There's not much anyone can do with those preliminary recordings. Maybe with the sheet music, but even that's not finished."

"Sheet music? Where would that be?"

Josh laughed a little. "Steve, for an old guy, was all about new technology. He used an app on his iPad to write sheet music, then stored the files along with the sound files. Find the recordings, and you'll find the sheet music."

Vanessa changed tack again. "Do you think Kathryn Sangster has a future as a singer?"

Fong still did not look at her, but his lips rose in a little smile. "Sure. With the right songs and the right band." He turned to her then. "And the right producer."

Vanessa nodded and picked up her shoulder bag. "All right. That's all, except for one thing. This studio is off-limits to non-police personnel, for the time being."

Fong started to protest but Vanessa cut him off. "So there's no contamination of a potential crime scene. If someone stole Mr. Sangster's songs, this studio will be material evidence. Thank you."

She watched him. He seemed to think about what she said, looked around the control room and reached for a computer keyboard. "Please, don't touch anything else," she said as evenly as she could.

Fong sighed, shook his head and stalked out of the studio, disappearing down the covered walkway toward the main house.

She turned off the lights in the studio and shut the door before heading in the other direction down the walkway. The rain was falling even more heavily than before, but the wind was no longer blowing it against her legs.

The walkway ended at a two-storey house. A staircase rose outside the walls, also covered. At a door below the stairs stood a man in coveralls. He was pulling the door shut. Kaholo Iolani, the groundskeeper.

"Mr. Iolani, I'd like to ask you a few questions."

He looked at her with open, deep brown eyes. *He's a handsome man,* she thought, *probably in his sixties, around the same age as Sangster had been.* Maybe a little younger, but in her experience, Hawaiian men often looked younger than their years.

"Okay," he said, closing the door.

"First, what's in there?"

He looked at her with a slight, amused smile. "Gardening tools." He pushed the door open again and flicked a light switch. Vanessa looked into what had to be the neatest, cleanest gardening shed she had ever seen. Rakes, hoes and spades hung neatly from hooks on the wall, a shiny riding mower sat in a corner, a green light indicating it was charging. A broom leaning against the wall had obviously just been used because the floor was spotless.

"Just locking up for the day," he said. "Can't do much else in this weather. Come on upstairs." He jogged up the wooden staircase on the outer wall. "Watch your step. It gets slippery in the rain."

The rain was letting up as Vanessa followed Iolani upstairs. The drumming on the roof over the stairs abated and the sky brightened just a little.

Above the garden shed was Iolani's apartment. *Compact and comfortable,* Vanessa thought as she scanned it. The door led into a small entranceway. On one side was a very manly looking living room, with leather sofas and more dark teak tables. It looked almost like a miniature replica of Sangster's living room, but one wall was all bookshelves, and they were filled.

The far wall held wide sliding glass doors that led onto a wide balcony. In the rain, Vanessa could not see whether it looked toward the ocean or the mountain.

A hallway led off the other side of the entrance, and Vanessa glimpsed a kitchen and more doors that presumably led to bedrooms.

Iolani held a hand toward the living room. "Sit

down. Give me a minute to change out of these dirty clothes."

"You did work around the grounds today?" Vanessa asked.

"There's things that won't wait," he answered as he disappeared into one of the back rooms. Vanessa heard drawers open and close, then the sound of a door opening, then water running. She took a moment to look at the books on the shelves. Histories of Hawaii. Big picture books of Hawaiian flora and fauna. Some biographies and a history of European exploration of the Pacific were all that Vanessa was able to see before Iolani returned, wiping his hands on a towel that he tossed into the kitchen. "What can I do for you?"

"How long have you worked for Mr. Sangster?" Vanessa asked, settling onto a sofa. It seemed to swallow her.

"More'n thirty years. He was my oldest friend, not just my employer."

"How did you first meet him?"

"He came out to buy this property. I was livin' down off Haou Road—you probly nevah heard a' it—"

"Haou Road? It may surprise you, but I have heard of it. I was doing an investigation on Haou Road last year."

"Really? Huh. Small world. Back then, thirty years ago, I mean, there weren't much on Haou Road. Not much there now, neither. Kine place. But I wuz lookin' for work. Steve wanted someone to look after the grounds. At first, there was a lot of work to do just to clear the land. It had just one house at the time. This one, in fact. So there was a crew of us at first, and we worked like dogs. Dat was when we first found the heiau. Boy, Steve got the stink eye from some of the locals. But he promised to give it to the people of Hawaii after he died, and they calmed down."

"How well did you know Mr. Sangster?"

"Like I said, he was my oldest friend. Let's just say the friends I had thirty years ago ain't so much friends no moah." He scratched absently at the inside of his elbow.

"You were close?"

"When I started livin' heah, that was befoah the current Mrs. Sangster showed up. He had just divorced Frances, his first wife and the mothah of Jeff and Janet. Once the big house and the studio were built, we didn't need a big crew no moah, so it was just him'n'me foah coupla yeahs. We did a lotta fishin' and a lotta doggin' aroun'. We both gets all buss up lots, too."

"You mean, binge drinking?"

"Sometimes. It da kine time, ya know?"

"That was when he gave you the original house to live in?"

"Just the top floah. We turn the bottom into that toolshed, like you see. I was the one what built the covered walkways between all the houses. Took me most a' five years to do dat. Big kine job for one man."

Vanessa paused. "I understand you were the one who found Mr. Sangster's body?"

"Yah, early dis mawnin. I was out on the property and I found him in dat kine pit behind the heiau. I knew right then he was dead, the way he was layin' on the ground like dat."

"Did you try to get him out?"

"No point. I come down, didn't feel no pulse nor no breathin'. So I took my cell phone an' call the cops."

Vanessa took out her notebook and jotted a few points down, even though the local police already had Iolani's statement. "When was the last time you saw Mr. Sangster alive?"

"I told the Hana cops it was last night, after dinner."

Vanessa wondered about the choice of words. "Is that not true?"

Iolani sat down on the sofa across from Vanessa and leaned close. His voice was low. "No. I saw him later las' night. He was walkin' around the grounds befoah the rain started. The moon was shinin'."

"Why was he out at night? Working on some songs?"

"Nah. He was talkin' with someone."

"Who?"

"I couldn't be sure. A man. I was thinkin' at first it was Kefir, but it was dark. To tell da truth, it look more like Jeff."

"Show me where you saw them."

Iolani led her out the sliding doors onto the balcony. It was covered and wide enough that the rain did not come into the house, but the edges were wet. From the orientation, she knew that one side of the view would be the ocean.

Kaholo led her to the side and pointed, up the mountain. "It's hard to see in this weather, but they were walking up there. It sounded like they was arguin' about something."

Vanessa looked where Iolani pointed. The rain had nearly stopped, and she could see across the neatly cut lawn to the trimmed edge of the rain forest. "Is the heiau that way?"

"Kinda." He moved his arm a few degrees. "More that way."

"But they could have been going toward it?"

"Sure. I guess at some point, Steve musta."

"What would Kefir and Steven have been arguing about?"

Iolani looked at her carefully for a moment, then looked up the mountain again. "The rain's almost stopped. I gotta pair a' slippahs that'll probly fit you if you wanna come see."

"Come see what, Mr. Iolani?"

He smiled at her. "You gotta look. And call me Kaholo."

He led her back inside, shut the sliding doors and went to a closet. "Here. Wear these so you don't get your nice shoes even more wet." He handed her a pair of rubber flip-flops that looked like they would fit.

Ignoring her further questions, he led the way out the door and down the steps again. Vanessa had no choice but to follow. Outside, the rain had stopped, but gusts blew fat, chilling drops off the roofs and the trees as they walked across the grass.

They didn't walk toward the heiau, but more steeply uphill, past a thick stand of sugar cane gone wild, then past bushes with long, tapered leaves. Finally, they came to an opening in the rain forest. The ground was covered with knee-high plants that Vanessa recognized immediately, even in the failing light. "This is a hemp grove, Mr. Iolani."

"Yup. It's Kefir's."

"These plants are for producing marijuana."

Iolani nodded again.

"It's a lot for one person. Did Mr. Sangster know about it?"

"Sure. He didn't mind, so long as Kefir let him have as much as he wanted. Steve believed that weed should be legalized."

"I know that. But this is still too much for personal use, even for the whole household."

"Yah. Kefir probly sells most of it."

"Did Steven Sangster know about that?"

Iolani was facing the hemp plants, but his eyes were not focused on them. "He knew and he didn't know, ya know? He didn't wanna know. But we all knew." He took a deep breath. "An' dat Keefer, he do more than weed. Pills, too."

"Why didn't you mention any of this to the local police this morning?"

Iolani looked at her intently, and Vanessa was suddenly aware of just how big the man was. He loomed over her in the shadow of the mountain behind him. "The local cops an' me, we have dat kine history. We're not friends."

"But you trust me."

"You wouldda found this sooner or later. I wanted to be sure you found da true story." He turned away from Vanessa, and she knew he was looking not at the fields of hemp, but at something in his own memory. "It's getting dark. We had better get back to the house," he said finally, turning down the mountain.

Vanessa trotted to keep up. "You said you thought the man talking to Steven Sangster might have been his son, Jeffrey. But that's not possible. He didn't arrive until today."

"Yah? Don't trust everything he say."

"Oh? Is there bad blood between you two?"

Iolani stopped and turned, towering over her again in the dark. She could not see his features in the twilight, but he bent over her, his broad shoulders blocking the sky. "That boy never respected his faddah. He always thought he was the smartest one in the room. When he took ovah managing Steve's finances and investments, he didn't do so good. He lost money, and he tried to make it back with risky investments. That didn't work out so good neither. But he nevah admitted it. He just keeps sayin' he's got all the answers. And he nevah wanted Steve to make no more records, neither."

"He mentioned that," Vanessa said.

"Did he?"

"He said he thought it would be 'another money loser.'"

"Yah, well, it's Steve's money, not Jeff's. Anyway, Steve nevah worried too much 'bout money. He nevah tol' Jeff dis, but he nevah gave the boy *all* his money. He kept enough to hisself to look after hisself."

Another lie from a dead man.

"How does that have anything to do with Jeffrey being here yesterday evening?"

"Someone came here in a rental car yesterday after supper. It was dark. Whoever it was left pretty late, just befoah Mrs. Sangster, Kathryn, come home. Today, Jeff brings his whole family here within a few hours of hearing about his faddah's passing. That's the fastest he ever got here from Wailuku."

"Is that strange, given he just heard about his father's death?"

"I'm jus' sayin' he never got here that fast befoah. When Steve have a heart attack las' year, Jeff took two days to come. Said his girls were at a recital or somethin'. So, yah, mebbe his faddah's death would be more motivation, but it seems strange for him."

"Are you saying Jeffrey Sangster killed his own father?"

Kaholo turned and continued on the way to the house. "All I'm sayin' is that he came here yesterday without tellin' anyone he was comin', and left again. And that was the last time anyone saw Steven alive."

"But you thought it could be Kefir."

Kaholo stopped again and looked at Vanessa over her shoulder. "I checked on that. Kefir was in his apartment, stoned out of his mind. There was no way he could have stood up, let alone walked around the estate after dark yesterday. It was Jeff, and if anyone asks me again, that's what I'm gonna say."

He continued toward his house, and again, Vanessa nearly had to run to keep up with his long strides.

Chapter 6:
An argument

Kaholo Iolani went up the wooden staircase to his own apartment, and Vanessa followed the covered walkway to the main house. Thunder rolled across the sky as the rain began again. *It's almost as if it deliberately stopped just long enough for Kaholo to show me Kefir's marijuana patch.*

A gust threw fat raindrops in the door before she could close it, but the next rumble was nearly drowned out by two women's voices.

In the kitchen, Mai stood with her hands on the counter behind her, as if she were trying to pull herself into it. Her wide eyes flicked back and forth between Erica Harrison, standing near the sliding doors to the deck, and Kathryn Sangster beside the table.

"No one needs you here," Kathryn shouted. "You're a has-been. You wanted Steven to help you with your comeback. Why don't you just get back in your fancy car and go back to Hollywood?"

"Steven called *me* to come here. It was his idea. I loved Steven. I still do. I don't need him to launch my career—unlike you," Erica retorted, tears on her cheeks reflecting the light from the lamp over the table. "News flash, Kathryn, you have no talent. You cannot sing."

"Go to hell, Erica," Kathryn snarled, her necklaces swinging as she pointed her finger repeatedly toward the former Mrs. Sangster. "Steve told me himself I have a special talent. The only reason you're sticking around is to get your hands on his money. *My* money."

"His money! If you knew the first thing about Steven, you'd never have thought of getting money out of him, you gold digging skinny bitch."

"Old hag!"

"Why are you attacking me? I lost my oldest friend today," Erica sobbed.

"*I* lost a husband!"

"It's not a competition, Kathryn!"

"Oh my god, the man's dead less than a day and you're already fighting over his money," Isabel West interrupted. Vanessa turned to see the personal assistant standing at the kitchen entrance. "Steven would be ashamed of you all."

"Shut up, you little tramp," Kathryn snarled. "You got no right to feel superior to anybody, not after you been sleepin' with my husband all this time." Isabel gasped, her hand at her throat.

"Woah, hey, what's going on here?" Jeffrey came in from the hallway, his wife right behind him. "Erica, Kathryn, calm down!"

"You shut up, too, you little weasel. You're the one who cost Steve the most," Kathryn yelled.

"Don't you call my husband a weasel, you bleach-blonde skank," Paula said, stepping around Jeffrey to advance on the current Mrs. Sangster.

"Bleach blonde?" Kathryn snorted. "No one uses more hair coloring than you, you stuck up, horse-faced psycho."

"Hey, that's my wife!" Jeffrey protested.

His wife took one more step toward the kitchen table and swung her arm, her open hand connecting with Kathryn's face in a slap that echoed off the walls. Kathryn staggered back, eyes and mouth wide open.

Paula raised her hand again, but Vanessa caught her by the wrist. "That's enough, Mrs. Sangster," she said, pushing the woman's hand down. "More than enough."

Janet, Sangster's daughter and her boyfriend, Kefir, ran up behind her, their eyes wide in curiosity and shock. When she heard Vanessa's words, Janet sobbed and covered her face with her hands.

"What's going on here?" said a commanding feminine voice. Lani Ferreira stood at the open patio doorway, fists on hips, lips drawn into a tight line, eyes burning, sopping wet hair dripping onto her shoulders. "Mrs. Sangster—Paula, that is—why did you assault Kathryn Sangster?"

"Assault? I didn't—" she began, but her husband cut her off.

"Detective, don't you think that's far too harsh a characterization of my wife?" said Jeffrey.

Lani ignored him. To Kathryn, she said "Mrs. Sangster, are you all right?"

Her eyes narrowed. "No. The little bitch hit me hard. I may want to press charges."

Paula gasped, her hand in front of her face, and Jeffrey said, "Kathryn, you can't be serious."

"Most of the Hana police detachment is here right now, Mrs. Sangster, and I can tell you no one is going to take your complaint this evening." Lani slid the patio door shut and tried to squeeze some of the rainwater out of her hair as she spoke to the crowd in the kitchen. "Normally, I would have the premises cleared as the whole estate is now a crime scene. But no one is going anywhere tonight in this weather. I'd suggest you all go to whatever rooms or apartments you have, and not interact with each other any more than absolutely necessary, until we can wrap this up."

"We were just hoping to get something to eat for supper," Jeffrey protested. "It's getting late, and my little girls are starving." A chorus of assent answered him. Everyone was hungry.

Lani turned to Mai whose face was as wet with tears as Erica's. She was shaking in her corner, watching the argument like a kitten watching tigresses fight. "Is there something to feed the little girls?"

Mai looked at her blankly for a few seconds, then nodded quickly. "Fine. Mr. Sangster, you can make something to eat for your family. And

Janet—do you want to feed your kids, too? Good. I trust you two can cooperate for a while. When you've finished cooking, take your dinners to your bedrooms. Then Kathryn Sangster can get herself something to eat—"

"That won't be necessary, Detective. I'm not hungry."

"Of course not," said Janet, rolling her eyes.

Before Kathryn could retort, Vanessa took her by the arm and pulled her out of the kitchen, giving Isabel and Erica as much berth as was possible in the crowded room. Passing Officer Gilmour in the hall, she sent him to the kitchen to help Lani keep order, then followed the most recent Mrs. Sangster to her bedroom.

"I understand that the CSI team has been over this room, so you're free to live in it. For your own sake, I suggest you stay here, away from the rest of the household until tomorrow, or whenever this storm breaks."

"I'm expected to grieve all alone with no one to talk to?" Kathryn sat on the edge of the king-size bed, fingers of one hand splayed across her chest.

Vanessa took in the room with her peripheral vision while pretending to focus on Kathryn. It had been recently redecorated. The window coverings and bed covers were new, she could tell, and the redecorating choices had not been made by a man. The few framed pictures were all of Steve and Kathryn together, and there were no pictures of Sangster's children, nor any of Steven and his musician friends. Those were all in the office or the studio.

"Do you like anyone in this family, Kathryn?" Vanessa found herself saying it, even though a voice in her head told her not to.

"What? Why, of course, I love them all."

"Of course." Vanessa turned away to leave. "If you do feel...hungry later, I'd advise you wait a couple of hours before going back to the kitchen."

"You're probably right." From somewhere—*It could not have been a pocket because those pants are way too tight to put anything in a pocket,* Vanessa thought—she produced a tissue and wiped a stray tear. Vanessa suppressed any thought that the widow was faking her grief, and in a second Kathryn sat down on the edge of her bed, covered her face with her hands and sobbed loudly. Tears poured between her fingers. She sobbed again, and then shaking her head moaned, "Oh, Steve. Steve, oh Steve."

Vanessa sat beside her, a hand on her shoulder. She said nothing, but let the widow cry it out. Finally, Kathryn lifted her head from her hands and took a deep breath. She blew her nose and when Vanessa gave her more tissues, wiped her eyes.

"I know what they say about me," she said in a hoarse voice. "I know that they think I'm nothing but a talentless gold-digger who slept her way into Steven Sangster's recording studio. But let me show you something." She opened a drawer in her makeup vanity and pulled out a folded sheet which she handed to Vanessa.

"Steve wrote this to me before we were married. I had just performed my first paying gig in Nashville."

The sheet bore letterhead from a Nashville hotel. The note below the crest was written in an elegant yet masculine longhand, dated some ten years earlier.

Miss Green,

Has anyone ever told you that you have a unique voice?

To say that I enjoyed your show tonight would be not just an understatement, but an injustice. I was blown away.

Yours is a special talent, one that only comes along rarely. And at this stage of your career, it is a voice that demands nurturing, care.

A music career is a hard road. Do not let the hangers-on, the ambitious and the commercial money people tell you different. Hold onto your dreams. Persist. I promise you, if you stick to your guns and sing the way that only you know best, you will succeed.

—Steven Sangster

At the bottom of the letter was the hotel's street address, and beside that, a three-digit number.

Vanessa did not need to ask what that part

meant.

"'Course, Steve wrote that in his drinkin' days," Kathryn said. "But for a twenty-year-old aspiring artist, it meant more'n the world to get a letter like this, handwritten by the biggest name in country music. At the time."

She went to a sideboard near the window and poured herself a double bourbon. She drank it all down before she turned to Vanessa again. "Would you like a little ..." she held up the bottle of Wild Turkey.

"No, thanks. I'm on the job." She stood. "I will have to leave you alone now. I understand how you must feel, but in an hour or so, get yourself some food to soak up some of that bourbon."

Back at the kitchen, Officer Gilmour and Detective Ferreira had organized feeding the household. Jeffrey and Paula were eating pasta with their three daughters, while Mai stood at the counter, eating noodles from her plate. "When they're done, it's Janet's turn with her boyfriend," said Gilmour. "Erica Harrison will eat with them, too."

"What about the officers?"

"Most of them have gone home already."

"I hope they live close by," Vanessa said as a gust rattled the patio doors. "I wouldn't want to drive the Hana Highway in this weather."

"We're all local," said Gilmour. "That being said, I wouldn't mind getting home myself. I have three kids and a fourth on the way."

"Wow," Vanessa said. "Sure, get going. There's not much more we can do here tonight."

As Gilmour left, Lani told the Sangster family not to go into Steven Sangster's office or studio. Then she and Vanessa went out the front door and ran to Lani's vehicle, a silver Toyota Tacoma. Vanessa jumped in and slammed the passenger door at the same moment that Lani closed the driver's side.

"Ruined," Vanessa said, squelching her toes together. Water oozed out of the top of the shoe.

"Are those Vince Camutos?" Lani asked, admiring Vanessa's shoes.

"Well, they were. I promised myself that if I caame to Hana again, I'd wear practical shoes."

"I always do," Lani said, showing her black Nikes. "Nice shoes just don't make sense in this job, especially here on the rainy side of the island. But I know the Bureau dress code."

Chapter 7:
Trading notes

Even though it was only a mile to the village of Hana, Lani took more than ten minutes to drive there in the rain. The wind was strong enough to shake her truck, and when they finally parked at the Travaasa Hotel, the biggest in town, they both hesitated before running through the downpour into the open concept lobby. By the time they reached the desk, they were both drenched.

A half-hour later, checked in, showered and dried, they sat in the hotel's restaurant. Vanessa had a glass of wine in front of her, Lani a pint of beer. They were off the clock, waiting for their meals, but they couldn't help talking shop.

"What did you get out of the interviews?" Lani asked just as a thin blond girl with colorful tattoos down her arms put their plates in front of them. Vanessa waited until she was out of earshot to answer.

"Mostly that everyone is lying," she said. "Everyone I spoke to is hiding something."

"How do you know?"

"I can always tell."

"Like Daredevil?"

"The superhero? No. Everyone gives off little signals when they lie. It's caused by stress."

"Like looking away or covering their mouth?"

"Those are two. But there are other common signals, too."

"Couldn't that just mean the person is feeling stressed? In a case like this, there are lots of reasons to feel stressed."

"It's not a perfect system, but it's usually pretty reliable."

"So, how did you develop the ability, if you're not Daredevil?"

"I studied it in university, and kept up my studies since. I have a bachelor's degree in clinical psychology from the University of Vermont, Burlington and a master's from Columbia."

"Wow. Well, I can't argue with that. But I got the same feeling as you—everybody on this estate has something to hide. The widow, the current Mrs. Sangster, seemed to be more angry at his death than sad about it."

"She let out a lot of grief when I was alone with her," said Vanessa. "Maybe she's more angry at the family than at her husband. Her late husband." She took a bite of her fish. *I love Hawaii,* she thought. "It's too bad we had to stop that argument. Some interesting facts came out."

"I thought so, too. Like Kathryn calling Isabel a tramp. Do you think she really was sleeping with Steven Sangster?"

Vanessa nodded. "Without a doubt. She

admitted to me that she was in love with him, had been since she was a teenager."

"That figures. That's why she came out here from the mainland—to work with her childhood hero and heartthrob. Sangster was really handsome when he was young."

"I remember," Vanessa smiled and sipped her wine. She thought of the one time she had seen Sangster play, in a club in New York City, part of a comeback tour—and a real comedown for a star who once packed the country's biggest stadiums. He was still handsome, then, close to fifty years old, but still with those rugged features, thick dark hair and beard streaked with grey, and those amazing blue eyes that seemed to pierce the heart of every woman in the audience.

"I remember, too. Too bad his son didn't seem to inherit any of his looks," Lani said.

"What do you think of that shot at the heiau? Was someone shooting at us or at Jeffrey?"

Vanessa heard Lani's phone chime, and she pulled it from a pocket in her jacket. She looked at the screen and said, "The crime scene investigators haven't found anything in the way of a discharged or missing shotgun. They checked all the guns in Sangster's collection, especially the shotguns," Lani said. "Either none of them had been fired, or if it was, it was cleaned really well and then coated in a fine layer of dust."

"So that means the weapon that shot at us is

not one of the collection. Of course, the shooter probably wouldn't have had time to return the gun to the collection before we got back to the house."

"Not necessarily. We took some time to get back to the house from the heiau. They might have had time. Or, the gun could have come from outside. It could have been someone else's gun."

"It could. We have not searched all the buildings, yet." Lani took a bite.

"What did you get from the widow?"

"Mostly that she didn't like anyone else in the family, and that Steven had promised to make her a singing star in her own right. And now that's not going to happen. Like you said, more angry than sad, although she was crying when she was by herself.

"Isabel West told me that Sangster was working on a comeback album, but all the recordings and backups are missing," Vanessa continued. "Do you think that's what all this is about? Someone taking his songs to pass off as their own?"

"You're thinking of the wife," Lani said.

Vanessa shrugged as she felt her own phone vibrate. "Maybe, but not exclusively."

"Who else?"

"I don't know. But they could try to sell them to someone else." She took her phone from her pocket, a text from Perry. "Still stuck in Honlulu arpt. Bd wthr. Sry." *Perry and his texting abbreviations,* she thought. The phone buzzed again as another text arrived. Vanessa frowned as she tried to decipher it. "CUTomw." What? Oh— 'See you tomorrow.'"

"Sorry, but that seems like a stretch," Lani said as Vanessa mentally composed a reply to Perry's text. She really did not need Perry trying to rekindle their romance while she was trying to solve a case during a tropical storm. "It seems to me there's more money to be made with the 'last recording by the late, great Steven Sangster.'"

"Maybe that's it: he was killed to drive up sales of his last album. It worked for John Lennon and Michael Jackson," Vanessa said.

"Except Michael wasn't deliberately killed."

"That's not what some of his fans say. But his death certainly brought him back into the public eye, and surely had an effect on sales of his last album."

"So you're thinking it's a beneficiary of his estate—one of his children," Lani said.

"Here's something. Jeffrey Sangster seems very defensive. He asked whether he's being accused of anything. He's already thinking about his inheritance."

"Already? The man's dead not even two days, and he's already thinking about what he's going to inherit?" Lani said. "More than one of the rest of the family said he made bad financial decisions for his father."

"I got that, too," Vanessa agreed. "He said his

father was going to leave the house and grounds to him, and he was concerned that if Steven ran up a lot of debt, that would leave him with nothing."

"Really? Janet said Steven told *her* he would leave her the house, except for the heiau, which he would turn over to 'the Hawaiians.'"

"That's not the only contradiction. Even though most people think that Kathryn is a hack singer, she showed me a letter where Steven said she blew him away. But not even Fong, the sound engineer, thought much of her musical ability. Not only that, but Jeffrey said his father wanted him to administer the entire estate, but then Isabel said he wanted her to fire Fong and manage all of his music and the money it made."

"So who's lying? Fong, Isabel West, Jeffrey or Janet?"

"Maybe Steven Sangster?" Vanessa suggested.

"A lying dead man? That's a first."

"Steven Sangster wouldn't be the first man to lie to his wife," said Vanessa. "There's one more person we haven't spoken about: Kefir, or 'Kiefer' Steinberg, Janet's live-in boyfriend. Kaholo Iolani, the groundskeeper, showed me Kefir's marijuana plantation at the back of the property."

"Really?" Lani cocked her head, then gave a half smile. "Growing weed in Hana is practically a neighborhood ordinance. Cops here look the other way when it comes to that."

"This was a lot bigger than a local patch in your backyard for personal consumption. He's supplying someone."

"He was supplying Steven Sangster," said Lani. "He told me himself he was toking with Steven last night."

"Really? So they got along, then."

"Weed has a way of making men friends," said Lani.

"Still, Kefir must be selling most of his crop to someone else. Which means there's a distributor."

"Sure. But there's not necessarily any connection to this case." Lani took another bite. "What else did you find out from Kaholo?"

"Confirmation of what we observed. Kefir's a deadbeat. Iolani also thinks he's taking some kind of pills. Maybe opioids."

"That's the second time I've heard that word today," Lani said. "One of the reporters in front of the house this afternoon mentioned a rumor connecting the Sangster household with illicit opioids in south Maui."

"A rumor? Do you know whether there's anything to it?"

Lani shrugged. "First I've heard of it. Frankly, I think that the reporter is just trying to create a name for himself."

Vanessa nodded, filing the idea away for later. "Iolani told me one other thing. Jeffrey mismanaged his father's money."

"Erica said he wouldn't let Steven spend money to promote his last two albums," Lani said.

"Kaholo also said that he thinks he saw Jeffrey walking with his father near the heiau last night," Vanessa said.

"What? That doesn't make sense. He only arrived this afternoon with his whole family."

"Unless he came out here last night to talk with his father and drove back at night."

"He drove the Hana Highway at night, then returned the next morning? That's a pretty tall order."

"But not impossible."

Lani nodded. "You do realize that the only place in the house for someone to shoot at us at the heiau is Kaholo Iolani's balcony?"

"I *did* notice that," Vanessa said.

Their dinner over, the women said goodnight. Vanessa watched Lani leave the lobby as she waited for the elevator. When the bell rang, she turned and jumped when she saw a woman standing beside her.

"Ms. Keahi? You startled me." That almost never happens. "When did you get here?"

In answer, the Hawaiian woman handed her a large manila envelope.

"What is this?"

"It is for you from Steven."

"I don't understand," she said, but took the envelope. It was sealed.

"Steven left this with me a year ago, after his illness. He said that, when he died, he wanted me to give it to the person in charge."

"In charge of what?"

"In charge of finding the truth."

"But I'm not in charge of this investigation."

Sophia smiled her little, mysterious smile. "Oh, I think we both know you are." She turned and walked away.

The elevator bell rang again, making Vanessa look toward the opening doors. When she looked back, Sophia was gone.

But Vanessa still held the envelope.

In her room, she first fired up her laptop before she tore the envelope open and dumped the contents onto the little hotel desk. There was a thick bundle of papers, folded and clipped closed.

She recognized it before she read the formal lettering of the title, "Last Will and Testament of Steven J. Sangster."

Four small items rolled out. Vanessa pushed them to the side.

Finally, a single sheet of lined paper, with notes written in a script that Vanessa recognized.

She read that first, but it was meaningless, a list of words, many just collections of random letters, followed by a string of numbers. But she knew what it was, *credentials and passwords for computer files.*

But what computer files? Stored where?

Are these his missing songs?

Is this another Steven Sangster collection of hidden meanings, like his earliest songs?

She could resist the temptation of the will no longer, and unfolded it. She scanned past the initial legalese about Sangster being of sound mind and in possession of his mental faculties. She read to find out who would receive what.

The name of the executor of Sangster's estate made her blow out a deep breath. *Sophia Keahi.*

Just who is this woman?

The provisions of who got what, however, told Vanessa who was lying.

Steven Sangster.

Last, the four small items were white tablets. Vanessa knew she would have to send them to the lab in Honolulu, but had no doubt what they were.

Opioids. Someone was *distributing opioids from Sangster's home.*

Sangster wanted someone to do something about it, but did not feel that he could.

But this was not the time to gloat over cracking the case. Time was clicking toward a deadline.

She spent the requisite five minutes of waiting for the hotel's limp wifi to get her to the FBI's network, and another five going through the multiple layers of security and identification. Finally, she opened the training module.

"Supervisory Skills for Police Superintendents" was the course that Vanessa had signed up for—was it three months ago, already?

She thought it would have taken her no more than a month to do the reading and the assignments, but work—actual investigative work—kept getting in the way.

Be honest with yourself. You put off opportunities to do the exam before because you hate exams.

She skimmed through the required reading. *Nothing that surprising. Nothing that doesn't make sense.*

On to the module exam. The passing grade was 80 percent, which would allow her to move onto the next training module and keep her in the stream for promotion in the Bureau.

The questions were easy, the answers obvious, because they were designed to be. Still, the slow network meant that Vanessa fretted over clicking her choice for Question 50, then waiting for the system to calculate and confirm her passing grade, before the midnight cutoff.

She needn't have worried. The screen showed her results at 11:37. She clicked "Accept and send to supervisor," then wrote a quick email to King.

Take that, Human Resources.

Chapter 8:
In the studio

The rain had stopped overnight, leaving the sky dark with clouds, the ground puddled and leaves hanging low. By 7:30 in the morning, Vanessa and Lani sat at a table beside the window in the hotel's restaurant, drinking coffee and munching on breakfast pastries.

"How long have you been with the Bureau?" Lani asked. She wore a different light jacket from the day before, over a pastel colored t-shirt. She had piled her curly hair into a bun and secured it with bobby pins, but the humidity twisted the curls that escaped around her face.

Vanessa was dressed in a light version of the Bureau "uniform": blue jacket, blue pants and a cream-colored silk blouse. Today, she wore her Mephisto walking shoes, which had a chance of surviving Hana's weather.

"Four years since I graduated from the Academy. I jumped at the chance of a posting in Hawaii. In fact, I think I replaced you when you left the Oahu station." Lani nodded. "Then Special Agent in Charge King assigned me to the Maui resident office in Kahului last month. On a six-month rotation, that is."

"How is King?"

"You probably know him better than I do. He makes a show of being 'by the book,' strict. But underneath that, he is a sweetheart. With a bit of a roving eye," she added.

Lani laughed wryly. "Yeah, a real teddy bear, most of the time, but he has a tendency to ogle when he thinks no one notices. But he's not hard to handle."

Vanessa decided to take a small chance on her new friendship with her predecessor in the FBI's Hawaii section. "Did King push you to do Human Resources' training courses?"

"All the time," Lani said, rolling her eyes. "And some of them are so *lame*."

"'Leadership' and 'initiative.' I know," Vanessa agreed, relieved that Lani had not defended the courses. "Some are good, and I know that they're part of advancing your career. But what I don't like is the time pressure. I had to do an exam before midnight last night, or I wouldn't be able to advance to the next level for I don't know how long. It would be a ... whole *thing*. But what I hate most are the exams."

Lani looked perplexed. "Well ... you gotta have exams. How else would you know you've learned the material?"

"Actually, exams are a poor indication of learning, worse for retention of information," said

Vanessa. Even to her, it sounded like an answer she had given many times before. "Sorry," she said. "My dad's a college professor. He always said he didn't believe in exams, but he still put a lot of pressure on me to excel at them, growing up. Lots of lectures and strategies."

Lani looked like she was trying to think of a response when her cell phone trilled. She answered, her frown deepening with every second. "Got it. We're on our way." She ended the call and stuffed the last of her muffin into her mouth. "Let's go. There's a new situation at the Sangster household."

Vanessa took one last slurp of her coffee and stood. "What kind of situation?"

"Isabel West is dead. Local officers are already there, and the coroner is on his way."

They trotted out to Ferreira's silver Tacoma, Vanessa gobbling down her croissant. Gusts destroyed her attempt at some kind of hairstyle.

Vanessa tucked her computer bag behind her knees in the front seat as she pulled the door shut. "Do you have more details about Isabel West?" Vanessa asked as she scrambled for the seat belt. Lani had the truck rolling before Vanessa could buckle in.

"Just that the cook, Mai Pham, found her body very early this morning. Kaholo Iolani called it into the Maui station," Lani answered, eyes scanning the highway.

"Mai found the body? Poor girl. She was

terrified when I spoke to her yesterday. Finding a dead body is tough." She repressed a gruesome memory, refused to let it take shape, but it was there at the back of her mind. She forced herself to think of Mai, the tiny cook, pressing against the corner of the kitchen as if she were trying to escape the strife among the wives and children of Steven Sangster the night before.

"It's something you never get used to, especially if you know the person," Lani answered, and Vanessa detected a bitter tone in her voice. *Is that evoking a painful memory?*

Her phone trilled, and Vanessa swiped the screen without looking at the caller ID. "Storm," she said, expecting King.

"Hey, babe, I found a way to make it to Maui," said Perry Boyd in his silky, deep voice. "I cannot wait to see you again."

"I told you, I don't have time for this," Vanessa snapped. When she noticed Lani's quizzical look, she thought about opening the passenger door and throwing herself out.

"Don't be like that, baby," Perry said. "Don't worry about anything. The weather's getting better, and I have found a way to get to where you are from Honolulu. So just hang tight, okay?"

Vanessa turned away from Lani, looking out the window at the green slopes down to the bluest ocean in the world. "I said, don't bother. I am in the middle of something very important and very sensitive. Don't call again until I call you. Do you understand?" She ended the call without waiting for a response.

"Everything okay?" Lani asked.

"Some people don't understand the difference between professional time and personal time," Vanessa said, hoping that Lani would drop the subject. *Perry couldn't have picked a more embarrassing time to call.*

With the rain over, the drive back to the Sangster estate took only a few minutes. Vanessa quickly told Lani what she had learned the night before about Sangster's real will, entrusted to the mysterious Sophia Keahi.

"That Sophia Keahi," Lani commented as she dodged between the media vehicles at the intersection of the highway and the access road to the Sangster estate. "I've encountered her before. She seems to know everything that happens in Hana. But talking to her is like talking to a Greek oracle. You never get a straight answer."

When they reached the Sangster estate, they saw that the group of media vehicles lining the access road had grown by two. Vanessa noticed a white van with a satellite dish on top that had not been there the night before. Only when Lani maneuvered past it could she see the E! logo on the side. *Interest is growing*, she thought. She wondered whether the reporters who had been on site the day before had maintained their vigil through the night.

The driver's door on the dilapidated Kia opened. The scruffy reporter stuck his head out and looked at them hopefully, and ducked back into his car when Lani did not stop.

Lani pulled her truck up behind two pickup trucks bearing Maui PD markings. The front door stood wide open;, a burly uniformed officer Vanessa had never seen before standing beside it. As she stepped past the threshold, fat raindrops hit the ground. Thunder grumbled somewhere off the coast.

In the living room with the view down to the ocean, Mai the cook sat on the edge of one of the sofas, looking at the floor and holding a tissue to her face. Officer O'Flynn sat beside her with a box of tissues.

Officer Gilmour came from the hall that led to the kitchen. "Sergeant Ferreira. Agent Storm. This way." He led them along the covered walkway to Sangster's studio, where another officer stood beside the door.

Inside, John Reid and Sheree Patel were already in the room, measuring, taking photos and notes. On the guest sofa under the window to the control room was a shape that Vanessa could not quite identify, not until she recognized the mid-high heels on the floor.

Isabel West's body slumped on the sofa. One arm hung limp over the side, the other folded across her body. Duct tape wrapped around her neck, holding a big, heavy-duty clear plastic garbage bag over her head, which was flung back. Vanessa could not help glancing up, as if the body were looking at something attached to the ceiling.

The plastic distorted Isabel's face. Her eyes were wide open, her jaw slack, the tongue protruding, thick. Her black hair, pressed between her head and the plastic bag, was a shapeless mass.

"Someone tried to pull off the duct tape," said Lani, pointing to the side of Isabel's neck, where a couple of inches of tape hung loosely.

"Mai tried to save her," Gilmour said.

"Who called it in?" Lani asked.

"Kaholo Iolani, the groundskeeper," Gilmour said.

"Where is he?"

"I asked him to stay in his apartment until you got here. Everyone else is either in the kitchen, or their bedrooms, still. Jeffrey and his family are in one of the suites upstairs. I haven't seen Kathryn Sangster yet this morning, but Officer O'Flynn says she hasn't come out of her room, yet."

"It's just past 8 a.m. I'm not surprised," Vanessa said. She felt fatigue like a heavy blanket over her shoulders and the backs of her hands.

"When did this happen?" Vanessa asked, indicating the dead body.

"The coroner hasn't got here yet."

"Why did the cook come to the studio?"

"I don't know," Gilmour answered, looking

embarrassed.

"Let's get out of the CSI techs' way," Lani suggested, and they went back to the living room. Mai was still on the sofa, but she wasn't crying anymore. She looked up at Lani and Vanessa, pain etched around her eyes.

"I'm very sorry about this," said Lani, crouching down in front of the small woman. "I know this must be very hard for you, but we need to ask you a few more questions."

Mai said nothing, gulping down more tears. Her eyes went from Vanessa to Lani and back. She blew her nose into a crumpled tissue and nodded. The corners of her mouth, pulled down, trembled.

"I understand how you feel," Vanessa said. "I remember the first time I found a body. It's something you never forget. But you will be okay."

"What time did you find Ms. West?" Lani asked.

"A little bit after seven o'clock," Mai said in a trembling squeak.

"Tell me what you saw," Lani prompted gently.

"It was Miss Isabel on the couch. I thought she sleep. Then I saw the plastic bag on her head. I try to pull it off but it holded on with tape." Her speech accelerated until the words tumbled out of her mouth, falling over each other. "I try to pull off the tape. I see she not breathing. Then Mr. Kaholo tell me not to touch her, to call police."

"Mr. Kaholo was there?" Vanessa asked.

"No, not until after."

"Sorry, I don't understand. When did Mr. Kaholo get to the study?"

"He come in after me."

"Why?"

Mai shrugged. "Maybe he hear me scream."

Lani asked the next question. "Why did you come to the studio so early?"

"I always get up to make breakfast for Mr. Kaholo. He get up early so he can do some work before day get too hot. I take him a tray, to his apartment, and I see door to studio was open."

"All right," said Lani. "Then what happened?"

"I look in studio. I see something first, I not sure what it is. So I come in and then I see Miss Isabel. I think she sleeping, so strange. I never see her sleeping before. But then I see the plastic on her head. I drop the tray and I scream. Mr. Kaholo come then. He say not to touch Miss Isabel. We came to kitchen and Kaholo call police. They come right away. Officer Sam come first. He take me here and tell Mr. Kaholo to stay in his apartment."

Gilmour had followed procedure, separating and isolating the two witnesses immediately until the police could take their statements without giving them an opportunity to discuss it among themselves.

"Who's with Kaholo Iolani?" Lani asked Gilmour.

"Officer Kana," he said, and Lani nodded as if she thought that were suitable.

They all turned toward the hallway at the sound of a child whimpering. Down the stairs came Paula Sangster. She carried her youngest daughter, who was trying to work her way up to a good cry. Behind her came her two other daughters, looking sad and sleepy, still wearing pajamas under jackets, and Jeffrey Sangster bringing up the rear, struggling to carry three suitcases.

"Where are you going, Mr. Sangster?" Vanessa asked.

"It's not safe here," he said, not looking at Vanessa. His oldest daughter turned toward him, eyes wide in alarm at the words "not safe here."

Paula stopped by the front door, shushing and bobbing the little girl in her arms. Jeffrey tried to put the suitcases down, but dropped them and they fell on their sides. He reached past his daughters and wife to open the door.

"Someone took a shot at me yesterday and barely missed," Jeffrey continued. "Now there's a killer in the house. I have to protect my family."

"I understand, but I cannot allow you to leave Hana."

Jeffrey looked at her, eyes as wide as his daughter's. "Why not?" He stepped closer to Vanessa and said in a low voice that Vanessa had to strain to hear, "Is there someone in my family you suspect?"

"You are a witness in a homicide investigation.

You can move your family to a safe location like a local hotel, but we will need to talk to you."

"Fine. That's where we'll go." Paula started to say something, but Jeffrey uncharacteristically cut her off. "We'll be safe at a hotel. Can we get some police protection there?"

"I'll ask the lieutenant in charge of the Hana station about arranging a police detail at the hotel," said Lani.

Jeffrey indicated with his head toward the front door. He hoisted the suitcases again and struggled out the front door, his wife and daughters following like disobedient ducklings. They had almost made it to their rented sedan when seven reporters, sound technicians and camera operators came charging up the access road, microphones out, all shouting questions at once.

Jeffrey and Paula turned as one and ran back up the front steps, pushing their girls ahead of them. Jeffrey pushed them inside and slammed the door, leaning against it. "Well, that's no safer," he panted.

"Maybe we can go to the guest house," said Paula. "As I suggested earlier."

"How would that be safer?" Jeffrey argued.

"We will be the only ones there," Paula said, her Spanish accent stronger. "We will know when anyone comes or goes, and the police are close by."

Jeffrey looked at her, mouth a thin, grim line. "Fine," he said and turned to Lani. "We're staying in the guesthouse," he announced. "We'll be isolated. Vulnerable. I demand 24-hour protection for us in the guesthouse."

Thunder crashed and the rain came down hard. The house got immediately darker and Lani found herself talking louder, over the noise of the rain hitting the ground.

"I can have someone monitor the guesthouse overnight, but I can't promise twenty-four hour surveillance until I talk to the lieutenant. In the meantime, Officer Gilmour, would you go to the guesthouse and show the Sangsters the basics of home security?"

"Yes, Sergeant," Gilmour answered, and went out the door, turning to a covered walkway that led to another two-storey house higher up the mountainside. It looked small compared to the main house, until Vanessa realized it was at least as big as some family homes back in Burlington, Vermont.

Jeffrey scowled, looked at his wife, who scowled back. He opened his mouth as if to say something, closed it again, picked up the suitcases and followed Gilmour.

Paula picked up her youngest daughter, and the two other sad little girls trailed her.

"We can't hold them without a warrant," said Lani.

"I know," Vanessa answered. I'll call King to see if we can get one quickly." She turned to Officer

O'Flynn, who was still sitting beside a quiet Mai. The cook was watching with wide eyes. "Kathryn Sangster hasn't come out of her room, yet?"

"Not that I know of," O'Flynn answered.

"Wait outside her room. When she comes out, take her to the study. Tell her what happened, but don't let her talk to anyone else. Right now, we have to interview Iolani." She turned to Lani. "Coming with me?"

"You go ahead. I'll go with O'Flynn to talk with Kathryn Sangster."

Lani ran up the stairs, Officer O'Flynn on her heels. Rounding a corner at the top, she saw Fong shutting Kathryn's bedroom door, straightening his shirt with one hand. "Mr. Fong?" she said.

He froze, looking at her with wide eyes, eyebrows climbing to his hairline. "Oh. Yes, I was about to come down to talk to you. I was ... just checking on Kathryn."

"You're close to Mrs. Sangster?" Lani asked.

"She ... she's a friend."

"A good friend, I think. How is she?"

"She's fine. She just wants to be alone."

"Where is your room?" Lani asked, striving to keep the edge out of her voice.

He pointed across the hall. "Right there."

"Step out of the way, Mr. Fong," Lani said. As she stepped past the sound engineer, she smelled wine and perfume—a woman's scent. She opened the bedroom door and stepped inside, conscious of

Fong still standing at the doorway, watching her.

"She's very upset—" Fong began as Lani closed the door.

Kathryn Sangster sat on the unmade bed, still in her housecoat. Her hair was a mess and she wore no makeup. On the nightstand were a wine bottle and a wine glass, half full. *Awfully early for wine.*

"I am sorry, Mrs. Sangster, but I have to tell you there has been another death in your home."

"Yeah, yeah, I heard all 'bout Isabel Wesht. Too bad, so sad."

"Is everything all right, Mrs. Sangster? Is there anything you need?"

"I have contacted counsel." Kathryn stood up, a little unsteady, and approached the door. "My attorney will be here as soon as possible. Until then, I don' wanna talk t'you." She pushed the door closed in Lani's face.

But before she did, Lani saw a second wine glass lying on its side, mostly under the bed. *Interesting.* She stepped into the hallway.

"Where did Fong go?" Lani asked Officer O'Flynn.

"Downstairs. I told him to go to the study."

"Come on," Lani said, and took the stairs down, two at a time.

Officer Kana, a muscular young Hawaiian man in what would have been a crisp uniform anywhere but in Hana's humidity, stood at the bottom of the staircase to the apartment above the garden shed.

Vanessa nodded at him, then ascended the stairs and went in without knocking. Kaholo Iolani sat at his kitchen table, his hands resting on top of a spread open newspaper. At one side was a tall, steaming mug. On the other, white smoke rose from the tip of a cigarette resting in an ashtray. Outside the window behind his bulky shoulder, grey sky darkened by the second.

He looked up as Vanessa and Kana stepped through his door. "You took your time getting here," he said.

"We understand you called it in," Vanessa said without preamble.

Iolani picked up his cigarette. "Yes, just like yesterday. Gotta say, the local cops respond faster'n you feds." He took a deep drag, flicked the ash off the tip and picked up the coffee mug in the other hand.

Vanessa stood across the small kitchen table from Iolani. "Do you normally get up this early, Mr. Iolani?"

"Gardeners always get up early. It gets too hot to work outdoors in the afternoon."

"Even in this weather?"

"It's hard to change the habits of a lifetime," he said, sipping more coffee. "Am I a suspect for some reason?"

Vanessa sat on a kitchen chair. "It's just that you showed up at the scene awfully quick."

"So you like me for this," he said. Vanessa wondered where he had picked up that particular bit of police slang. "Mai always bring me breakfast. She's a sweet girl. But she was a bit late today, which isn't like her. Then I heard screaming from Steve's studio. When I got there, Mai was trying to pull the plastic bag off Isabel's head. I told her not to touch anything until the police got here. That's it."

"What happened next?" Vanessa asked. As she did, she saw a flash through the window. A few seconds later, thunder rumbled.

"Big kine commotion," Iolani said. "Jeff and Janet came running to the studio, then most everybody else in the house. I pushed them away, back to the kitchen. Know enough 'bout cops not to disturb a crime scene." He shook his head. "Poor Isabel. She was a sweet kine girl."

The wind hit then, like a monstrous fist against the side of the house. Rain flooded down, distorting the windows and drumming against the walls.

Vanessa took a long, deep breath. "Tell us about her. Did she have any enemies? Anyone who would want to harm her?"

Iolani laughed and picked up his cigarette, now almost gone. "Sure. Kathryn Sangster."

"Why? Was Isabel sleeping with Steven?" Lani asked.

"God, yes. She was crazy 'bout him. She been

bangin' Steve almost from the first day she come here."

"Did Kathryn know?"

"I don't see how she could *not* know. Everybody knew. 'Cept maybe for Mai. But mostly, Kathryn didn't wanna know."

"Is Kathryn still in her bedroom?" Vanessa asked Kana.

"Kathryn likes to sleep in most mornings," Iolani said, stubbing out his cigarette. "She stays out most nights, partyin' with her girlfriends."

"Does she have many friends in Hana?" Vanessa asked.

"Couple. Real bitches, you ask me."

"I can go see if she's up," Officer Kana offered.

"If she hasn't woken up with all this going on, I'd be amazed," said Vanessa. "Mr. Iolani, please don't leave the premises until one of us has a chance to talk to you again."

He held his hand toward the window. "I ain't goin' nowhere in this," he said. "I don't think you are, neither."

Vanessa and Kana left Iolani's apartment, making their way along the walkway which was awash from rain blown in from the side. The sky was dark grey.

Vanessa worried about ruining even her hiking shoes. "Did anyone actually verify that Kathryn Sangster was in her bedroom?" she asked Kana, raising her voice over the noise of the rain drumming on the cover over the walkway.

"I don't know. Do you think she killed Isabel West?"

"I'm not saying anything like that. We don't have enough information, yet. But if she's not actually in her room, but has left the estate, it would reinforce that hypothesis."

They found Officer Gilmour in the kitchen, munching on a piece of Portuguese sweet bread as Mai looked up at him, waiting for approval. "This is good," he said, chewing on the side of his mouth. "Really good. What do you call this?" Then he saw Vanessa and Kana come through the sliding doors, and his face reddened. "Detective," he mumbled. "I thought Mai was pretty shook up, and maybe if she had something to do, it would take her mind off things."

Vanessa cut him off. "Where are the Sangsters? Jeffrey and his family, I mean."

"I went with them to the guesthouse and started to explain some security procedures, but they kicked me out."

"Okay. Is Kathryn Sangster still in her room?"

"Lani went to talk to her," Gilmour answered.

Janet Sangster, wearing pajamas and a fluffy robe, came into the kitchen and collapsed onto a wooden chair. Her eyes and nose were red, her cheeks puffy. "Oh, my god. It's just awful," she said, her voice hoarse. "Who would hurt Isabel?"

Mai put a mug of milky coffee in front of her, and she took a noisy gulp.

"I'm so sorry for your loss," Vanessa said. "Were you close to her?"

"She was my friend," Janet whispered hoarsely. "And that's a horrible thing to happen to anyone." She leaned closer to whisper even quieter. "I haven't told the kids, yet."

Vanessa recoiled. Janet still had morning breath, overlaid with coffee and milk. "Come and see me in the living room when you're done with breakfast. I need to talk to you. And where is Kefir?"

"I guess he's still in our apartment," she said.

"Bring him," Vanessa said. "We have to talk to everyone again."

Janet picked up the coffee and shuffled out of the kitchen.

Lani and O'Flynn came in. "Where is Josh Fong?" Lani asked.

"I haven't seen him," said Vanessa.

Lani pressed her lips together. "I just saw him coming out of Kathryn Sangster's bedroom. I told him to come down here."

Interesting, Vanessa thought. "Can you talk to Erica about Isabel?" Vanessa asked.

"Gladly," Lani said.

"Don't let her talk to Janet before I have a chance to."

"I got that," Lani said, and took off down the hallway.

Vanessa started to leave, but Mai tapped her arm. The diminutive cook looked up at Vanessa with big, troubled eyes. She did not say anything, but looked around—out the sliding doors where the rain continued to thrash the deck, then back to the hallway. "You looking for Josh Fong?"

Vanessa looked closely at the small woman, seeing fear, but underneath it, strength. "Yes. Do you know where he is?"

"He went out before you come into kitchen today," she said.

"Where did he go?"

"Out the big doors," she said, pointing to the sliding patio doors.

"Where was he going?"

"I not know. He not say."

"In the rain?"

"He wear raincoat." She stepped closer to Vanessa. "I have tell you something about Josh."

"What is it?" Vanessa said, bending a little to hear her quiet voice.

"Do not tell him I told you this, please?"

"All right. I'll keep this confidential, as long as I can. But I can protect you as the source, Mai, if you know something that implicates Josh in a ..." She tried to keep her words as simple as she could, given Mai's command of English. "... a crime."

Mai checked the walkout and the hall again before gesturing Vanessa closer. She whispered something that the FBI agent could not hear.

"What was that?" She bent lower.

Mai stood on her toes and whispered into

Vanessa's ear. "His name not Josh Fong. He not American. He Vietnamese. Like me. His name Lahn Ngo. He used to live in Honolulu."

"How do you know this, Mai?"

"My friend know his cousin. He very bad man. Have trouble with police, go to jail one year." The young woman was shaking. "Very bad man. Drugs. He hurt people."

"Have you told anyone else about this?" Mai shook her head. "Did Mr. Sangster know?" Another shake. "All right, Mai. Thank you for telling me this. It could be very important. Now don't worry— I can protect you."

Mai was trembling even harder now. "What's wrong?" Vanessa asked.

"I very scared."

"Don't worry," Vanessa said. "You have been very helpful, and I can help you. I promise."

A flash of lightning threw the kitchen into bright exposure, illuminating every fine strand of Mai's hair for a moment. Then thunder shook the house. A light bulb burst with a pop and a second flash, and the house dropped into darkness. Mai screamed and threw her arms around Vanessa.

"It's all right. It's just a power outage," Vanessa said, patting the small woman on the back of the head. She heard a faint whine, and a second later, the lights came back up, flickered twice, then stayed on. "See? Everything is fine."

It took several minutes, but Vanessa eventually

extricated herself from Mai's clutch. She hustled to the living room. Through the big window, she saw a Chevy Suburban with Maui County markings pull into the array of vehicles near the road. A short man climbed out, carrying a large briefcase over his head against the heavy rain, and ran up the steps. When he opened the front door, the wind slammed it against the wall behind it and blew in enough rain to leave a puddle on the hardwood floor.

"Busy couple of days here at the Sangster estate," he said at the door as he shook the rain off. He was short, with narrow shoulders and a round, protruding belly. He put down the briefcase, revealing a bald head circled with an untidy fringe of hair, and held out his hand. "I take it you're Special Agent Storm." Vanessa detected a hint of a British accent. "I am Dr. Kanvir, the county coroner for southern Maui." He wiped rain off his wire rimmed glasses with his shirttail. "As every one of the assistants is busy, I have come to collect the body."

"I can help you with that," said Officer O'Flynn, walking in from the verandah. All efficient energy, she led him to the studio.

It was a little past nine a.m. when Vanessa speed dialed King's mobile. He answered on the second ring. The hollow quality to his voice and some background noise brought Vanessa a vision of the florid King driving his convertible—with the roof up, if Honolulu's weather was anything like Hana's today—talking into the microphone hanging from his ear buds. She quickly brought him up to speed on Isabel West's murder, as well as what she thought so far.

"Good move on keeping the wife isolated. But try to talk to all the others before they start sharing stories with each other."

She pressed the button to increase the volume because it was hard to hear him over the rain. "We're on that."

"I know I promised you some more resources, but Terakawa won't be able to get to your location today," King added. "With this weather, there's not a plane nor a boat that's going to make the trip from Oahu to Maui, especially not that tiny port in Hana. As soon as the storm breaks, he'll take a chopper. In the meantime, be careful. Do everything strictly by the book. I don't have to tell you how high-profile this is."

"I'm surprised we're not already swarmed by media," said Vanessa.

"I guess you can thank the weather for that, at least. Keep me in the loop, Vanessa." Lightning flashed close and the phone line crackled, then went dead.

Janet came into the living room, now dressed, with her hair brushed. "What did you want to talk to me about?"

"Where's Kefir?" Vanessa asked.

Janet swallowed before she said, "I don't

know."

"What? He left? When? How?"

"I said, I don't know." Janet flopped onto one of the overstuffed chairs. "I can't find him anywhere in the house. Unless he went to the studio or to Kaholo's house. But he wouldn't do that."

Officer Gilmour came into the room then, speaking into the police radio microphone pinned to his shoulder. "Yes, sir." At the same moment, yet another police SUV pulled up in front of the house, parking on the access road that led to the Hana Highway, blocking the vehicles already at the house. An officer in a hat and slicker came up to the house as lightning flashed again, followed by thunder a few seconds later.

Rain followed the policeman into the house. When he took off his slicker, Vanessa recognized the rank markings on his uniform. "Good morning. Agent Storm?"

Vanessa nodded. "I'm Lieutenant Matthews, in charge of the Hana Station," he said, his voice low and gravelly. He was short for a cop, burly, with crew-cut blond hair that made his head look flat.

Vanessa shook his hand. "Pleased to meet you." She turned as the lieutenant's eyes focused behind her shoulder. Lani Ferreira came from the kitchen, Mai hurrying behind her with a mop and bucket.

The three cops moved into the living room. Lieutenant Matthews held his belt in both hands in front of his ample belly as he got straight to the point. "Detective Ferreira, this investigation is taking up a lot of my resources," he said. "The Hana station is short-staffed as it is, and you've got three officers here that are needed in the community."

Matthews continued as Gilmour came down the hall, pulling on his slicker and putting on a hat. "We've got an accident on the Hana Highway by Kawakoe Gulch and another call at Hana Bay. I'm going to have to pull some officers off this detail."

"What about the guard on Jeff Sangster and his family?" Lani asked.

Matthews shook his head. "Sorry. I just don't have the manpower. I can leave you with Officer O'Flynn to help with this investigation. But I need everyone else for our normal operations."

"Well, that definitely does not help," said Lani after they had left.

Vanessa turned to Janet. "When did you first hear about Isabel West's death?"

Janet looked up at Vanessa and Lani, her chin trembling. Tears brimmed in her eyes. "I heard screaming. It was Mai. I ran to see what it was. Everybody was outside Dad's studio, yelling and screaming." A tear spilled down her cheek.

"Was Kefir with you?" Vanessa asked.

"He was right behind me." Janet nodded.

Vanessa sat down on a sofa facing Janet.

"When you say 'everybody' was outside the studio, who do you mean, exactly?"

Janet took a deep, shuddering breath. "Mai was there, crying. Kaholo was shouting for everybody to stay out of the room until the police got there."

"Who else was there?"

"Jeff came. Paula, too. Erica."

"What about Josh Fong?"

"Umm ... I think so."

"Close your eyes, Janet," Vanessa prompted. "Relax. Picture the scene in your mind, just the way it happened. Look from left to right. Now tell me, who was on the walkway in front of your father's studio?"

Janet closed her eyes. "Jeff. Erica. Paula behind her. Mai. Kaholo in front of the door. Kefir behind me." She thought more, biting her lower lip. "No. Josh was not there." She opened her eyes. "But he came later. His apartment is farther from the studio than mine."

"How many damn apartments does this house have?" Vanessa mused aloud.

"Seven, including mine. Mine's the biggest, with room for the kids. Eight if you include Kaholo's, but it's kind of separate. Then there's the guesthouse."

"Rock stars," Vanessa muttered. "All right, you say you saw Josh. Where?"

Janet hesitated again. Suddenly, the room lit

up as lightning flashed over the coast. A second later, thunder rattled the windows. Janet screamed and even Lani jumped.

"Where did you last see Josh Fong, Janet?" Vanessa repeated.

"I guess ... in the kitchen. He just came in, poured himself a cup of coffee and left again without saying anything."

"Was that before or after the police got here?"

"Umm ... after, I think. I was just starting to make something for Ben and Madison. That was after Officers Gilmour and O'Flynn came. Yes, I'm sure they were here."

"Do you think that Josh might be with Kefir right now?"

"Uh—probably not. I mean, they're not really close friends or anything. Not that they don't like each other. They just don't normally hang out."

"Not even to smoke pot?"

Janet blushed bright red. "What do you mean?"

Vanessa almost laughed. "Don't worry—we're not looking to arrest someone for growing weed in the back forty, not during a murder investigation. But could they be working together on moving Kefir's marijuana crop?"

"I—I wouldn't know anything about that," Janet said, icily. She stood up. "Do you have any other questions, Ms. Storm?"

"We better find Kefir and Josh Fong," Vanessa said.

"I'll call in a Be-On-Lookout for them," said Lani. "They can't have gotten very far in this weather. No one could."

Another flash and crash of thunder, nearly simultaneous this time, made everyone in the room jump. At that moment, an ambulance appeared at the end of the driveway. It reversed, beeping, maneuvering between the police vehicles as close as it could to the house. Two men wearing rainsuits and hoods got out. They took a stretcher and a large black bag up to the house. Officer O'Flynn and the coroner, Dr. Kanvir, led them toward the back of the house and the walkway to the studio.

Lani and Vanessa followed them onto the wraparound verandah at the back of the house. They peered into the murky haze of the pouring rain toward the garden shed. "Is someone there?" Vanessa asked.

"Where?" Lani asked.

Vanessa pointed toward the garden shed. "I thought I saw someone out there."

"Who would be walking around in this weather? I don't see anyone."

Vanessa stared for a minute longer, but her eyes could not penetrate the gloom and the rain. "I don't know. Anyway, I want to take a look at Sangster's computer files. Maybe there's something there that can help make sense of this case."

Chapter 9:
Hidden meanings

In the study, Vanessa settled herself again behind Sangster's massive desk and clicked the computer to life. While Lani conferred with the crime scene techs in the studio, Vanessa searched for anything she could see that might be useful on the computer.

Nothing interesting in the emails. There were exchanges with record companies, mostly routine royalty statements. *No new information.*

She saw an exchange between Sangster and Erica, where he invited her to come to Hana, but the messages were professional, mostly empty of any personal connection. She saw the attachments in the Sent folder, thirty-second excerpts from songs. She opened one and the distinctive sound of Steven Sangster strumming on a guitar filled the study. Vanessa found herself nodding in time to the music before it ended.

She searched the file structure, skipping over the financial folders for now. *Let the forensic accountants go through that if it turns out this is motivated by the inheritance.*

Eventually, she found a folder labelled "EH."

Erica Harrison? She double-clicked on it, to be answered by a new window asking for a password. She tried a blank password, but the box just shook and asked again. She tried "password," "Erica" and a few other obvious combinations, but nothing worked.

From her computer bag, she pulled out Sangster's mysterious handwritten note from the envelope Sophia Keahi had given her the night before. Scanning the nonsensical list, she found one entry that began EH. She copied the digits beside it on the computer.

The folder opened to a list of text files. She double-clicked one labelled "Investigator."

Great. Song lyrics.

A song with another hidden meaning?

"A man may suspect his friend

"Shares his bed when he's not there.

"The woman he loves and the man he trusts

Bends his art to steal his heart."

God, this is terrible. I hope this isn't one of the songs he sent to Erica Harrison.

If these are hidden meanings, they're not even as well-hidden as his early songs.

She scanned down, looking for something she could use.

"A friend keeps me in leaf"

Pot?

"But what he does on the side, the company he keeps"

Okay, does he mean Kefir? Is Kefir his friend? Or someone else?

She scanned lower.

"...white bitter candy he sells sends the young To early more bitter oblivion."

So was Iolani right about the pills? Opioids?

She clicked back to the list of files, opening another with the information from Sangster's list.

This was not a bad poem, though. It was a simple instruction.

"Open the book, Atlas of Maui. Top shelf, bookcase beside the desk."

Vanessa found the book and put it carefully on the desk. As she reached to open the cover, she felt a tingle in her fingertips. Her hand hesitated, as if by a mind of its own.

She scoffed and flipped the cover open. *If Sangster wanted to hurt a cop, he would have done it by now.*

She found a cliché she would never have expected from a poet like Steven Sangster. The pages inside had been carefully hollowed out in the middle to leave a square, paper cavity. Inside the cavity, a small, resealable plastic bag.

And inside that, six small whitish round pills.

Just like the ones in the envelope yesterday.

Under the bag, a loose scrap of paper with two words, written in the same handwriting as the list.

She went back to the computer and opened the root folder, then a subfolder matching the first word on the paper scrap. With the second word as the password, the folder opened.

The contents were not text files, but photos.

Photos of envelopes of baggies of whitish pills on a table.

Some photos of bags of pills, stuffed into what looked like waterproof sacks, the kind that canoeists used.

The last picture in the file was not of pills, but a boat with an outboard motor. And at the wheel, a slim man with dark hair.

Josh Fong.

Vanessa went back to reading text files and looking at pictures, but there was nothing that gave her any more information.

She searched for financial files, anything that might provide context beyond her own guesses. But every other folder was password protected, and none of Sangster's codes worked to open them. Eventually, she gave up. She would need to find someone who knew the password, or get a technician who could hack through it.

Chapter 10:
Storm in a storm

Vanessa found Lani talking with a teary Erica Harrison in one of the countless guest rooms. Lani summarized her interview for Vanessa. "She hadn't heard about Isabel West until I told her."

Erica dabbed at her eyes with a tissue. "I heard some noise, but I didn't want to get in the way," she said. "I'm sorry I can't be more helpful."

"That's all right," said Vanessa.

"Do you think I can go to the kitchen to get some breakfast?" she asked.

"I'm sure that will be fine," Vanessa said. "Thanks for your cooperation. One more question, though. When was the last time you saw Josh Fong?"

Erica shook her head. "The sound guy? Yesterday evening, some time."

"I'd like to talk with him. Do you have any idea where he might have gone?"

"None at all. I don't know anything about him. I only just met him yesterday."

Vanessa thanked her and returned to the kitchen, the last place any witness had seen Josh Fong. On the way, she passed what the Sangsters called the "games room." It had the biggest television she had ever seen and a stack of games, consoles, as well as a pool table and a complete home theater. She glanced in to see Janet's children, Madison and Ben, playing a first person shooter game. Ben's character killed Madison's, and she howled "No fair! You cheated!" as her brother laughed.

Janet came in then, ordering her children to turn off the television. "We're on the generator now. We have to save power." The kids moaned and protested, and Vanessa moved on before seeing how the argument would play out.

Thunder rolled again when Vanessa came into the kitchen to see the glass door slide open. Through it stepped Kefir Steinberg, wearing a nylon jacket with a hood. Water dripped from his shoulders and arms onto the floor and beaded his face. He slid the door closed behind him as thunder rolled again.

"Where have you been this morning, Mr. Steinberg?" Vanessa demanded.

"Out," he answered, standing still to let the water drip off him.

"You're trying to tell me you were just out for a stroll in a tropical storm?"

"I don't have to justify myself to you. I know my rights."

"You don't know them very well. Enough shit. Tell me where you were all morning."

"I was looking for something."

"Did you find it?"

"Yes."

"Care to tell me what it was?"

He looked at her through narrowed eyes for a moment, then unzipped his jacket and pulled out a satchel. He reached inside and pulled out the biggest revolver Vanessa had ever seen.

Her heart pounded. There was no time to reach her trusty Walther before he could turn that massive weapon toward her. But he put it carefully on the kitchen table.

It was an antique weapon—that was clear from the curved shape of the wooden grip and the fancy engraving on the cylinder. Where other revolvers had an ejector rod, under the barrel was a tube, bigger around than the barrel itself. And there was a strange external rod on a clip alongside the barrel. The bottom of the grip had an eye, as if it were meant to be hung on a nail.

"Where did you find this?" she asked.

"In the toolshed under Kaholo Iolani's apartment," he answered.

Lani came into the kitchen then. "Kefir Steinberg," she said. "I could arrest you for interfering with an investigation."

"What? Why?" he asked.

"You have moved evidence," Lani replied, stepping closer.

"I *found* evidence and brought it to you!" Kefir protested. "How is that interfering?"

"It would have been better if you hadn't touched this, but just told us about it and brought us to it," Vanessa said. "But if it's Kaholo's gun, he may have every right to own it."

Lani came to the table like the revolver was pulling her. Her eyes were locked on the weapon. "Wow. That is one old gun."

"I know. Kefir found it in Kaholo's toolshed. I've never seen anything like it before."

Lani pulled on latex gloves and picked up the gun. "This is very unusual. It has two barrels, one under the other." She held it so Vanessa could get a closer look.

"The hammer is strange, too. It has a little tab in the middle," Vanessa said.

"It's not loaded—you can see into the chambers from the front. And it's been recently cleaned. I'll get this to the lab. Maybe someone there can identify this gun."

"It looks to me like it's from the Civil War days," someone said. Lani and Vanessa turned to see Officer Corinne O'Flynn behind them, looking at the gun. "The cylinder is round. Cylinders in modern revolvers have indentations between the chambers, called 'flutes.' But older guns didn't have those. And see, it's made to be front-loaded." O'Flynn pointed at the chambers. "This was made before bullet cartridges. You had to pour powder into the chamber from the front, and hold it in place with wadding. Look — it has nine chambers.

Probably because it took so long to load, you wanted to have as many shots as possible on the battlefield. It must weigh a ton."

Lani and Vanessa looked at the uniformed woman. With her slender face, large, earnest eyes and bobbed chestnut hair, she looked more like a schoolteacher than a cop. Yet here she was, holding forth on an obscure, antique gun. "Was it Steven Sangster's?"

"It used to be," said Janet Sangster, who had returned to the kitchen behind O'Flynn. "He was so proud to find this at some antique gun show on the mainland. He made a present of it for Kaholo's sixtieth birthday."

"I think we should talk to Kaholo," said Lani.

"As soon as we secure this evidence," said Vanessa. "Mr. Steinberg, come with me." Lani put the big pistol into an oversized, clear plastic evidence bag and took out her notepad to log it.

Vanessa led Kefir to Sangster's study. She closed the door behind them and pointed him to a sofa. "Why do you suspect Kaholo Iolani?"

"Who says I suspect him?"

"I already told you to cut the shit. Why did you search the garden shed?"

"You cops had been everywhere else on the estate, except there. I saw you glance into it yesterday, but you didn't even go in."

"You were watching me?" Alarms rang in Vanessa's mind.

"No. I was watching Kaholo." Kefir's voice was

flat, expressionless.

He's hiding something again. "Why do you suspect him?" she asked again.

"I never trusted him since I first came here. Guy's a junkie, always sneaking off to shoot up. You can't trust junkies."

"You're saying he's a heroin addict?"

"That's what I'm saying. I know the signs. The scratching, the skin wounds, the dopiness and sleepiness. I could tell right away. So one day I looked into his apartment window and saw him shooting up."

"You're quite a spy," said Vanessa dryly.

"Look, do you mind if we talk later? I'd like to get into some dry clothes."

"Go, and come back as soon as you've changed. And if you leave the house again before I tell you it's okay, I'll arrest you. Got it?" As if to reinforce her point, lightning flashed again, making the lights in the house flicker.

Kefir swallowed, looking at her as if gauging whether she was serious, then nodded.

Going from the study toward the stairs to the bedrooms brought them past the front entrance, where Jeffrey Sangster burst through the front door, carrying his two younger daughters. Paula carried the oldest right behind him. Jeffrey's clothes and shoes were wet, but Paula was drenched from head to toe. Her hair hung over her shoulders, dripping, and mud covered her pants and shoes.

As Kefir went upstairs, Vanessa confronted the five dripping Sangsters. The youngest daughter cried on her father's shoulder.

"Mr. Sangster? Why are you back here?"

"We're not staying in the guesthouse in the dark. There's no electricity there, for some reason. At least here there's power and police officers. If someone's trying to kill me, I feel safer here. We all do," he added after a look from his wife.

"Poppi, the rain hurt my face," said the oldest daughter. "The wind was so strong."

"I'm sorry, honey. We're okay now. We're indoors and we're staying here until the rain stops," Jeffrey said, crouching down to his daughter's level and wiping rain and tears off her face.

There was nothing Vanessa could say. "Very well, Mr. Sangster. But your family will have to stay in your own rooms as much as possible and cooperate fully with the investigators—and that includes searches of your rooms. Understand?"

Lani came from the hall then, carrying the old gun in the clear evidence bag. Janet followed her. "Why do you have my father's antique gun?" Jeffrey asked.

"Please step away, Mr. Sangster. This is evidence," Lani said. "I'll put it into the study until we can take it to the station," she said to Vanessa.

"Is that what shot at us? My father's antique gun?" said Jeffrey, trying to follow Lani into the study until Vanessa stepped in front of him with her palm raised.

"I don't think so, Mr. Sangster. It's a revolver, not a shotgun."

"That, Agent Storm, is not just a revolver. It's a LeMat Grapeshot revolver from the Civil War. It's a nine-shot pistol, and the cylinder rotates around the barrel of a shotgun. There's a little lever in the hammer that you can flip up to change from firing bullets to firing shot—or a slug. It was one of my father's favorite collectibles until he gave it to Kaholo as a birthday present. Where did you get it? I haven't seen it in years."

"Josh found it in the garden shed," said Janet.

This is exactly what I was afraid would happen when conducting an investigation in the middle of the crime scene, Vanessa thought. *Not only was this potential evidence compromised, the witnesses were talking to each other, which made getting accurate statements from any of them almost impossible.*

Vanessa looked at Jeffrey, then at Lani, who was also staring at the singer's son. "Mr. Sangster, please step into the study with Sergeant Ferreira. Mrs. Sangster, will you please take your girls to their rooms? Thank you."

Paula's lips tightened and her nostrils flared. Cutting ahead of an angry tirade, Vanessa called down the hallway. "Officer O'Flynn—can you help Mrs. Sangster take her children to their rooms?"

Officer O'Flynn came from the kitchen, smiling at the little girls. Behind Vanessa, Lani tilted her head toward the study and led Jeffrey into it. Paula glared one more time at her husband, then turned, picked up her smallest daughter and followed Officer O'Flynn upstairs. The young Sangsters followed.

Chapter 11:

Interlopers

When she got back to the living room, Vanessa saw more headlights on the access road. A Jeep Wrangler pulled into the muddy parking lot. *This is ridiculous. We might as well put a revolving door in front.*

Two men got out: a short, pudgy man who pulled a blazer over his head to try to keep the rain off, and the driver in a hoodie. Vanessa recognized the long legs and broad shoulders immediately.

Outside, the two men ran up the steps and threw open the front door, adding to the flood on the floor. The shorter, pudgy man in the blazer carried a briefcase. His brown hair was just a fringe around his otherwise bald, lightly tanned head. Under his drenched jacket, he wore a muted Aloha shirt that was nearly as wet. His tan chinos and brown loafers were covered in mud.

Behind him, the driver pulled down the hood. Tall, athletic, African-American with a clean-shaven head and a stubbly beard, Perry Boyd gave Vanessa a look that somehow combined hope, apology and confidence.

"What are you doing here?" Vanessa

demanded.

The short man slipped a card out of his jacket pocket. "Allan Guzman," he said. "I'm Kathryn Sangster's counsel. I'd like to see my client immediately."

Vanessa looked at the card. Bloom & Fernand LLP, Attorneys, it read, with a Honolulu address, in plain white with a gold logo and embossed black lettering. It looked legitimate. "I'm sorry. I did not know that Mrs. Sangster had requested counsel."

"She called me late yesterday," the lawyer replied, shaking rainwater from his shirt. "She is under no obligation to inform you as she exercises her civil rights."

Vanessa sighed. "Of course. Go ahead."

"And you are?"

Vanessa showed him her credentials.

"Very good, Agent Storm. Can you direct me to my client? I have never been here before."

"Just a moment," she replied and turned to Perry. "You, sit down in the living room and don't dare move until I get back."

She led the lawyer and Kefir to the study, where Lani and Jeffrey were looking at the antique gun. "I'm leaving Steinberg with you for a minute. Don't let him out of your sight." Then she led Guzman to Kathryn's door. She knocked but didn't bother to wait for a response before opening the door. "Your attorney is here," she said.

Kathryn had cleaned up quickly. She sat in front of her vanity, wearing a loose, peach-colored blouse and beige slacks. Her hair was brushed, her makeup applied, and her huge earrings shone in the lamplight." Thank you, Agent Storm," she said, her voice clear and strong. She stood, hand extended to the lawyer. "I'm very pleased to see you, Mr. Guzman."

"Pleased to meet you, finally," he replied. "Sorry it took so long to get here. No one wants to go island to island in this weather."

"Well, I'm glad you persevered." Kathryn turned to Vanessa. "Thank you again, Agent. I'd like to discuss some things with my counsellor in private." She shut the door in Vanessa's face.

Perry was still standing in the middle of the living room, admiring Steven Sangster's guitar on its stand. "I didn't want to sit on the furniture while I'm all wet," he said. "I have some other clothes in my suitcase, but it's in the car, and I'll get even wetter if I fetch it."

"You cannot be here, Perry. This is a crime scene and I'm in the middle of an investigation."

Perry's smile turned into concern.

"You ignored all my texts and voicemails.'

"I told you, I'm very busy. You do know I'm an FBI agent, right?"

Perry smiled the halogen-bright smile that was the first thing Vanessa had noticed about him, years ago, and shrugged his broad shoulders—the next thing she had noticed. "You're so beautiful when you get all official like that."

"Stop it. How the hell did you get here in this weather, anyway?"

"It wasn't easy, let me tell you." That was a phrase Perry had picked up from her father last Christmas, and it annoyed her coming from Perry even more than from her Dad. "When I got to Honolulu yesterday, the weather got so bad that my connecting flight to Maui was cancelled. What's that airport called, C'thulhu?"

"Kahului," Vanessa corrected him.

"Yeah, well, all the flights and the boats were cancelled, too. I don't have a lot of time to kill on this trip. I gotta get back to California in a few days. But I found this other guy who wanted to get to Hana, too, so we split the cost of chartering a plane to Maui."

"You took a private plane? In this weather?"

"We hadda offer the pilot a lot of extra money to take us. Mile for mile, it must be the most expensive air trip I've ever taken. We left early this morning. The rain started again as soon as we landed, and once we rented a car, it took us, like, six hours on that little road they call the 'Highway to Hana.' That's, like, a local joke, right?"

"You do know the Highway Department recommends that people not drive that highway in a storm?"

"I just hadda see you." Perry held his arms out and stepped close, trying to embrace Vanessa.

She brought her arms up and stepped back. "This is so not the time for this. What are you thinking—to rekindle a romance while I'm at work?"

Perry lowered his arms, disappointed. He tilted his head and looked into Vanessa's eyes, the way she knew that he knew she could not resist. "If you had read any of my texts, you'd know that I had a meeting in Honolulu before the trade show, which I blew off. When I found I had a chance to travel to Hawaii, I couldn't *not* see you. Even you have to understand that."

"What's that supposed to mean—'even me'?"

"Ever the perfect professional federal agent." He stepped closer again, angling for a hug. "Come on, admit it: you're happy to see me."

Vanessa let him wrap his long, strong arms around her and indulged in his scent for just one magical second. Then she pushed him away, not gently but not roughly either. "This is not the time. I have to get to work. Now sit down and don't move until I get back."

She put her hand on the study doorknob, then turned, thinking of something. "Wait—how did you know I'd be in Hana? I'm stationed for now in Kahului."

"I went to your apartment first, then to the station."

"How did you know where my apartment is?"

"Your mom told me."

Vanessa closed her eyes to suppress a groan. Her mom, bless her heart, still trying to promote her love life.

"You do realize that my mother does not know why we broke up."

Perry put his sheepish look on again. "And I appreciate your discretion, baby."

"Don't 'baby' me."

"Sorry. And I know I made a mistake. A bad one. But I've learned from it. I've changed. And I want us to become stronger—"

"This is *not* the time for this conversation, Perry," Vanessa interrupted. She turned the doorknob, then froze. "Wait—no one at the station would tell you I was in Hana."

Perry smiled. "When you answered my call, I backtracked your physical location."

"You can do that with a cell phone?"

"*I* can."

Vanessa gave him her coldest glare. "Be careful, buster—you may have just admitted to a felony. Now seriously, sit down, shut up and for god's sake, don't touch *anything*."

She looked out the front living room window as an especially hard gust shook the house, and she heard a deep groan.

Vanessa groaned herself as she saw a big koa tree fall behind Perry's rented Jeep. It crashed, blocking the access road.

That will keep the reporters away, she thought. But it would also prevent anyone in the Sangster house, including Perry, from leaving.

Chapter 12:
Antique weapons

In the study, Jeffrey and Lani stood over the desk, looking down at Steven Sangster's huge, antique pistol. Both were wearing latex gloves, and Jeffrey was pointing out the gun's special characteristics. Kefir sat on a chair in the corner, looking sullen and bored.

Vanessa snapped on a pair of gloves and stepped closer. Jeffrey picked the gun up and pulled back the hammer to expose nine chambers. "It's a cap-and-ball, single-action revolver. You have to put a cap on each of those nipples. Pull the trigger, the hammer hits the cap, which acts as a primer to fire the charge in the chamber."

He pointed at the middle of the cylinder. "You see there are nine chambers in the cylinder? That cylinder revolves around a 20-gauge shotgun barrel."

Vanessa and Lani leaned closer to see the smooth center barrel. "What an idea."

"Back when it was invented, there were no bullet cartridges like we have today. You had to pour in gunpowder, push in wadding, tamp it down and put in a lead ball. The rod attached to the side is for tamping down the powder and wadding. Coincidentally, this model has a 20-gauge bore, and it can take some brands of modern shotgun shells. But like the revolver, the shotgun part was originally made to be barrel-loaded. There's no breech." He touched the end of the cocked hammer, which tapered elegantly. "See this?" He pushed it up, and the center of the hammer swiveled up, which caused the other end to swivel down toward a metal nipple over the end of the center shotgun bore. "That's how you fire the shotgun."

"Amazing. What an invention," said Lani.

"It was an interesting idea, but not very practical," Jeffrey said. He put it in Vanessa's hand. It felt three times as heavy as her sleek Walther. "It's a heavy gun, and like all barrel-loaders of the time, it took a long time to load. And those rammer levers kept breaking off. But it is an interesting gun for a collector."

"Tell me something," said Vanessa, trying to keep her tone casual. "Does Kaholo like this gun, too?"

"Oh, yah, he's an enthusiast. He liked it so much, my Dad gave it to him as a birthday present."

"When was that?"

Jeffrey shook his head. "Oh, I don't know. Must be about four or five years ago."

Lani took Jeffrey up to his guest room on the second floor, warning him to stay there and not to talk to anyone else. She knew it was not strict or

162

reliable protocol, but given the circumstances, where they were stuck in a big old house, cut off from police property or resources, there was little else she could do.

Vanessa opened her tablet computer and typed notes, as frustrated as Lani at the inability to access Bureau resources, or even Wikipedia. She wanted to know more about the LeMat grapeshot revolver.

But this could be the answer to what had puzzled them for the past two days—a shotgun shell fired at her, without a shotgun to be found. This LeMat shotgun disguised as an old pistol may be the answer, but she had no way of knowing for sure.

Kefir made noises to show he was impatient and bored, but Vanessa and Lani ignored him. Finally, Lani said, "Maybe we should interview Kaholo again. Now."

"You go ahead. I'll secure Kefir."

Lani left, head down as the rain drenched her even under the thatched roof of the covered walkway.

Vanessa directed Kefir ahead of her to his own bedroom, collecting Officer O'Flynn along the way. "Don't let him leave under any circumstances. Even to use the bathroom." She winked at the officer so that Kefir, standing in the open doorway to his room, could not see. "If he tries to leave, shoot him."

Kefir swallowed. Vanessa pulled his door shut and patted O'Flynn's shoulder as she went back downstairs.

The rain flew almost sideways, drenching her right side as she ran along the covered walkway. Vanessa held onto the banisters with both hands as she climbed the wooden outdoor stairs, and her heart hammered in her chest when she saw the open door. Her right hand reached under her soaking wet jacket for her gun as she stepped into the apartment.

Her breath left her audibly as she saw Lani, then caught again in her throat when she saw the body stretched out on the floor.

"I was about to call you," said Lani. Her eyes never left the man on the floor.

Kaholo Iolani lay on his side, one leg bent awkwardly under him, his arms splayed. His left sleeve was rolled up high to allow for a rubber tourniquet around his biceps. His skin was ashen, his fingernails black. His eyes were wide, staring at a point on the floor ahead of his right hand. His lips were open and black, and a puddle of vomit lay beneath them. His chest did not move.

Beyond his outstretched right hand lay a syringe with a needle. A spoon lay, bowl side down, near his bent left knee. White powder sat on a crumpled square of foil paper on a table beside the sofa.

"A setup," said Vanessa.

"You think?" Lani answered. She crouched down beside the body, still holding the antique revolver in its plastic bag, which she used to point at Kaholo's neck. Vanessa crouched beside her to see a thin line of blood from a tiny puncture. "Right in the artery," Lani said.

They stood, looking around. "Someone killed him and tried to make it look like an accidental overdose," said Vanessa. "Kefir told me that Kaholo was a longtime user, and that means he knew his limits."

"A long-term user is not likely to have overdosed accidentally," Lani agreed.

Vanessa looked around for any more clues, and a glint under a chair rewarded her. She picked up a small stud earring with diamonds and small green stones. "Look familiar?" Lani nodded.

Vanessa checked her phone. Lani was right, there was no service. "We can't phone this in, and there's no way for the coroner to bring a vehicle in here now, anyway. I think we should not announce this to the family for now."

"Keep it quiet so the killer doesn't know that we know? Good idea. Come on, let's get back to the main house. Shake the trees and see what falls out."

"Starting with Josh Fong. If we can find him."

Lightning flashed again, thunder booming seconds later. Vanessa frowned at her phone screen. "Well, it looks like cell service is back."

"Never mind that," Lani said, striding toward the main house. "Let's find Fong."

Chapter 13:
On the dock

Officer Sam Gilmour hated having to work outdoors during Hana's frequent downpours. This one, though, was more than just a shower. It was a real tropical storm, early for the time of year. And it was shaping up as one of the worst he had ever seen.

On the other hand, he needed an excuse to get out of the Sangster house. There were things more important than a stupid celebrity murder. Like a paycheck.

But first, he had to check out a complaint called in about something suspicious down at Hana's marina, he thought. He laughed at the term, "marina." More like a boat ramp with a jetty beside it.

"'Suspicious activity.' Probably some local kid saving his stash from the rain," he muttered to himself, peering through the downpour that obscured anything more than 20 feet ahead.

Keawa Place curved around the beach on Hana Bay to the end at the jetty. Smart boat owners had pulled their craft out of the water ahead of the storm, and they sat on the sand or on trailers, covered with tarps and looking miserable. When he realized he would have to get out of the car to check the boats, Gilmour wondered whether the Lieutenant hated him.

Behind the last trailer before the jetty was a small car, an old Toyota Corolla. Its color was indistinguishable in the dark. He shone his car's headlights on the license and jotted it down in his notepad before maneuvering his SUV around the compact car and continuing to the jetty.

He squinted forward at what might have been movement at the jetty, but it was hard to tell with the rain running down the windshield and the wipers constantly going back and forth.

"What the hell?" he muttered. There was someone there, all right. The phoned-in tip had not been a lie. He touched the gas, easing the vehicle forward. When he got to the jetty, he turned on the floodlight.

A slim figure froze in the sudden light but did not turn. As far as Sam could see, it was a man, a hood pulled over his head against the rain, bent over inside a small boat that had a deck and an outboard motor. As he pulled closer, Gilmour could see the man struggling to untie the boat from the dock.

He knew who it was. He eased the SUV onto the concrete pier, stopping at the metal gate that crossed it.

He put his hat with the plastic cover on before opening his door. The noise of the wind-driven rain hitting the bay and the pavement drowned out any sound that he could have made. The onshore wind lashed the rain into his face. He slammed the door and turned on his flashlight, even though it wasn't necessary with the car's floodlight. Cold rain seeped under the collar of his slicker and over his shoulders and chest.

He stepped through the gate onto the wooden boards of the jetty itself, pausing behind the man in the boat. "Give me the pills, Josh," he said.

Fong whipped around, squinting into the combined light from the car and Sam's flashlight. "Sam! I'm just trying to bring my boat onto shore before the storm wrecks it."

Gilmour drew his sidearm and squatted. He was still looking down on the sound engineer. "Cut the shit, Fong. Give me the pills."

Fong backed away, reaching for the key that would start the engine. "Pills? Sam, you have it all wrong. I am just trying to save my boat—"

Gilmour pointed his gun at Josh. "Get out of the boat, Fong."

He barely heard the roar of the motor over the sound of rain and wind. Fong pushed the control lever all the way forward. The boat lurched forward, sending the cop off balance, but the knots held and the boat bounced back. Sam snatched his fingers out of the way, less than a second before the boat crunched against the jetty.

But he did not see the fist coming for his face.

His back slammed onto the dock and his gun flew out of his hand.

He glimpsed Fong jumping out of the boat, long legs springing down the jetty and through the narrow gate. Gilmour scrambled to his knees to retrieve his gun, then sprinted after Fong.

The sound man ran past Sam's police SUV and toward the battered Corolla, and had too much of a head start for the cop to catch up. As Fong wrenched the car door open, Sam saw a backpack hanging off just one shoulder. Cursing again, Sam sprinted back to his own vehicle, his boots crunching on the crumbling, wet asphalt. He heard the Corolla start up with the telltale rattling roar of a blown muffler.

By the time he turned his SUV around, he could see the Corolla's headlights disappear behind the trees along the beach. The police vehicle fishtailed on the wet pavement as he stepped on the gas after Josh Fong.

He hit the radio button. "Officer Gilmour pursuing escaping suspect on Keawa Place, heading into Hana. Asian male in an old Toyota Corolla, color indeterminate."

He felt ridiculous calling in a suspect fleeing in an old car in tiny Hana. The dispatcher echoed the sentiment. "A speeding Corolla? Is that even possible?"

"It's happening," Sam said without pressing the Send button on the radio. Instead, he held the steering wheel with both hands as he followed the curve of the road around the bay. Ahead, the Corolla went around the bend to the left where Keawa Place turned to meet Uakea Road. He thought about requesting a roadblock. But then he thought about the value of the pills in Fong's satchel.

"Dispatching another car to Hana Highway south of the village," came the voice out of the radio. "But I don't know if they'll get there in time. The lieutenant and Kana are out at that accident near the airport."

"Good." Again, he did not press Send when he spoke.

At the corner of Uakea, he hesitated. Which way had the Corolla gone? On a hunch, he turned left, toward the Sangster estate. His guess paid off a minute later as he passed the baseball diamond at the corner of Hauoli Road, leading to the Hana Highway. Skid marks on the pavement curved to the right, and something had just taken out part of the hedge around the front yard of the big white bungalow on the corner.

Gilmour negotiated the corner more nimbly than the Corolla had, but he still felt the tires slip. Hauoli Road ended 200 yards farther, at the Hana Highway. And there was the Corolla, its front end firmly wedged into the low stone wall along the front of the white church across the road. The driver's door was wide open, and Sam saw a tall form running away, disappearing into the wet gloom.

He sped up. In seconds, the headlights and the spotlight that he had neglected to turn off caught Fong's running form.

The man looked back, his glasses reflecting the spotlight. He had one hand up beside his head. Gilmour pressed down on the accelerator. The slim man dodged to the side. Sam swerved to meet him, slamming on the brake when he felt the thump of Fong's body on the fender, then rocking as the front left wheel rolled over him.

Once the SUV had skidded to a stop, Sam reversed carefully until he felt the rear wheels roll slowly over the body. Then he got out into the horizontal rain. He did not need his flashlight to pull Josh Fong's body out from under his vehicle. He waited long enough to ensure the man did not breathe before pressing his radio button.

"This is Officer Gilmour. There's been an accident. Suspect is down on the Hana Highway, south of Haouli Road. Send an ambulance."

Then he saw the phone in Fong's hand. He pried it out and saw whom Fong had called.

"Shit."

Chapter 14:
Hemp takedown

Lani hated cases that involved celebrities. They all had to be treated so carefully. They were so thin-skinned, difficult and resentful of every little thing that the police asked them to do.

Standing beside the grand piano in the front room, she looked beyond the disordered cars in the parking lot, to the tree lying across the access road from the Hana Highway. Between the branches of the trees screening the property from the road, she could see the corners of some of the media trucks and their satellite dishes on the roofs. She thought of the reporters, camera people and sound engineers sitting in them, waiting out the rain, hoping for a glimpse of something.

"Good luck getting any clear photos in this weather," she said under her breath.

She stretched her neck and shoulders. She hadn't had a chance to run today and missed her workout. Sometimes, cases were like that.

She also hated cases that took her away from home overnight, and this one looked like it was going to stretch into yet another day in Hana. But given the rain, there was no way to commute here on the Hana Highway, which was treacherous enough in good weather. Which almost never happened on that twisting road—not for a full day, anyway.

At least the wind is dying down. Maybe this storm is finally ending.

Her thoughts went to the new FBI resident on Maui. Vanessa Storm was undeniably smart, if a little overconcerned about her wardrobe. She was someone that Lani knew she should try to cultivate a professional friendship with—smart, well-dressed, ambitious, driven—if perhaps a little introverted.

Which brought her thoughts to the discovery of Kaholo Iolani's dead body. She had told the FBI agent that, as a long-term user, the groundskeeper must have known his limits, and therefore was unlikely to have overdosed accidentally.

A conclusion Lani knew all too well.

The thought of Iolani lying on his apartment floor led inevitably to the memory of Lani's father. This time, she could not prevent the image of her father on the floor of the hovel where he had lived since Lani had been a child. He had been a long-term user, as well. Except that nothing else mattered to Luca Ferreira.

But Lani had never been able to dismiss the thought that maybe his last overdose had not been accidental. That maybe her father, the man she had not seen for years, had taken his own life.

A short blast from a police siren pulled her out

of her reverie. At the third wail, she saw red and blue lights reflecting off the wet leaves near the road. A Maui PD cruiser negotiated between the media trucks and stopped at the fallen tree. The lights went out, the headlights dimmed. After a moment's hesitation, the driver got out. Even in his long slicker and rain hat, Lani recognized the lanky form of Officer Gilmour. He flung a long leg over the trunk of the fallen tree and climbed past.

She met him at the door. "What's up? I thought Lieutenant Matthews needed you on the road."

He stood on the porch, which provided cover from the worst of the rain, and tried to shake off some of the water from his hat. "That problem is now resolved. Josh Fong tried to steal a boat but gave up when I saw him. He escaped and crashed his car on the Hana Highway. I'm sorry, but he's dead. Now, I need to speak with Kefir Steinberg."

"Dead? Fong is dead? Wait—what does Kefir have to do with that?"

Gilmour bent down and lowered his voice. "We believe he was involved in trafficking with Fong. Where is Steinberg?"

"He's in his room. Officer O'Flynn is watching him," said Vanessa, coming into the room. "Why do you need him?"

Gilmour drew himself to his full height. Lani noticed that his hand went to his sidearm.

"He's wanted for questioning in relation to the death of Josh Fong," he said.

Vanessa and Lani asked questions at the same moment. "You said Fong died in a car crash," Lani argued.

"Fong is dead?" Vanessa blurted.

"I have orders to take Kefir Steinberg in," Gilmour insisted, his voice breaking.

Vanessa indicated the stairs. "Bring him here. He's in his apartment in the guesthouse." After Gilmour had left, Vanessa said to Lani, "Stay on the verandah, in front of the door. I'll go around the other way to Janet's apartment."

"Why?"

"Gilmour is lying."

"Well, duh. Do you think it has something to do with the pills?"

"Let's see."

They tensed at a woman's cry, then another, then a man's and the sounds of crashing and stomping feet.

Officer O'Flynn drummed her fingers on the handle of her sidearm. This assignment, babysitting a stoner like Kefir Steinberg, was so boring it was giving her a headache. *I cannot believe a case involving a big star like Steven Sangster can be so boring.*

Boredom, and the headache, vanished like a soap bubble when Sam Gilmour appeared at the corner of the hallway, water dripping from his slicker to the hardwood floor. "Is that Kefir Steinberg in there?"

"Yes. Why?"

Gilmour shouldered past her, hand on his weapon. "I'm arresting him for murder."

He put his hand on the door handle when Janet Sangster ran into the hallway. "No! He's innocent!" she screamed.

Several things happened at once. Gilmour pushed the door handle down, then stumbled forward as the door was wrenched open from the inside. Kefir Steinberg leaped over the lanky cop, into the hallway as Janet crashed into O'Flynn, sending her sprawling.

O'Flynn managed to push Janet off her in time to see Kefir, wearing a yellow hoodie and a backpack, run out to the wraparound verandah, then onto the covered walkway to the guesthouse. Sam Gilmour chased after him, rain slicker flapping. She jumped to her feet and followed.

Vanessa ran around the verandah in time to see Kefir Steinberg leap off the covered wooden walkway to the guesthouse, landing in wet, thick grass. He sprinted away, up the slope toward the back of the compound.

Officer Gilmour leaped right behind him, followed by Officer O'Flynn, who landed on the grass inches behind the lanky cop.

"Lani!" Vanessa called, turning toward the front of the house, but the Maui detective was already vaulting over the verandah's railing.

Vanessa followed her onto the high grass.

The wind had died away and the rain was down to a drizzle, but the grass was heavy with water. Within a few long steps, Vanessa's pants were soaked up to her knees.

Kefir led the group around the main house, past the studio and then Kaholo's former apartment. Lani passed Gilmour, with Corinne closing in behind. Then Vanessa saw Gilmour slip and fall, and O'Flynn get tangled in his long legs.

Vanessa passed them, her longer stride bringing her closer to Lani.

Kefir reached the tree line and ducked under low-hanging branches, heavy with rain. Thunder rumbled and the sky flashed. The rain returned, hard as a shower.

Lani ducked under the trees, dodging hanging leaves and tangled roots, hoping she wouldn't twist an ankle on the uneven ground while she tried to keep an eye on Kefir's t-shirt as he fled. There was barely any light under the trees, and she lost her quarry for a moment.

She dashed into the jungle, wet branches slapping her in the face. *Where is Vanessa?* Then she heard her voice. "There, to the left."

Kefir was trying to evade them by changing direction. "You go straight, then come left," Vanessa said, and took off to the left, trying to outflank Kefir.

Lani ran ahead, following the faintest path,

hopping over logs and dodging roots. Wet leaves soaked her clothes and hair. She glanced over her shoulder to see Gilmour trying to make a beeline for the fleeing Kefir. Being taller with long legs and arms, he was having a harder time getting through the jungle, and was falling behind. But Vanessa ran through the forest as if she had been born to it.

Lightning flashed, illuminating Kefir's yellow hoodie to Lani's left. She turned and poured on as much speed as she could. She was closing on him, and beyond him, she could see Vanessa charging from the other side.

Kefir glanced toward Lani, then at Vanessa and changed direction again, in a vector between and away from his pursuers. Suddenly, they were out of the jungle in a clearing. Part of Lani's mind catalogued the knee-high hemp plants covering the cleared ground.

The rain hit them, so heavy it felt like a giant hand pushing down on her head and shoulders. As she closed on Kefir, it came down even heavier, obscuring her vision. Kefir slipped, stumbled and fell, sliding on the wet ground. He was up again in a second, but before he could take two more steps, he went down on his back.

Lani registered the sound of a gunshot a second later.

When she saw Kefir fall, Vanessa skidded to a stop, sliding on mud and crushed hemp. The rain drowned out any echoes of the gunshot. She ran again to kneel at Kefir's side, slapping both hands onto his thigh to try to staunch the flowing blood. Rain flowed over her head and into her eyes, but she could not wipe them clear.

Lani knelt on Kefir's other side a second later. "Who fired?"

They looked back to see Officer Gilmour holding his firearm down by his side. Between them and him stood Corinne O'Flynn, staring at Gilmour openmouthed.

"Why did you do that?" she demanded.

"He has a gun," said Gilmour.

"I didn't see a gun!" Corinne said.

"There's no gun," Lani called.

"I don't have a gun," Kefir groaned. He tried to sit up.

"Stay down. We have to reduce the bleeding," said Vanessa.

"Get over here and help," Lani ordered Gilmour. Slowly, the tall man approached. "What the hell is with you? Why did you shoot?"

"I thought he had a gun," Gilmour repeated. "He's a drug dealer. He and Josh Fong are the main distributors of illegal opioids in this part of Maui."

"No, we're not!" Kefir shouted, struggling to sit up again. "This guy is! He's been shaking us down for months. Now he shot me! And he killed Josh!"

"Shut up, Kefir," Lani growled. "I haven't read you your rights, yet."

"I don't care. You can't arrest me unless you arrest this asshole, too. He's the one who brings in most of the cody—"

Gilmour raised his sidearm to aim at Kefir again, but before he got halfway there, he was looking down the barrel of Vanessa's Walther. "Drop it," she said.

Gilmour hesitated less than a second before sprinting back toward the jungle. Lani sprang after him, tackling him before he reached the tree line. The two of them rolled over, crushing against hemp plants, until Gilmour slipped from Lani's wet grasp. He took off toward the trees.

Skidding to a stop, a burly uniformed cop in a clear rain slicker emerged from the tree line. Gilmour turned and started in the other direction, until O'Flynn delivered a kick to the back of his knee that brought him down.

"Stay down, Gilmour. Anything you say can be used against you," Lieutenant Matthews growled. Officer Kana came up from behind and snapped handcuffs on the renegade cop, then began reciting Miranda rights.

Vanessa pressed her hands on the wound on Steinberg's leg again as Matthews approached.

"Kefir Steinberg, you are under arrest. Do not move," Matthews said over the sound of pelting rain.

He crouched beside the wounded man. "You have the right to remain silent, and anything you say can be used against you in court. That being said, you have been injured. Detective, Agent, we have to get this man out of the rain and to some care."

Lani and Vanessa nodded assent.

"Can you stand?" Matthews asked. Kefir nodded, and Matthews helped the young man to his feet. "You're going to have to help him back to the house."

He turned to the big Hawaiian cop standing over Gilmour. "Bring him to the main house, too."

Lani pulled the pack over Kefir's back and slung one strap over her own shoulder. She and Vanessa each put one of his arms over their shoulders and slowly, awkwardly, they made their way across the hemp field, then through the thick forest to the Sangster compound as Vanessa recited Kefir's Miranda rights.

Chapter 15:
Wet

By the time the group got back to the compound, Vanessa and Lani were carrying Kefir between them. Officers Kana and O'Flynn flanked the handcuffed Gilmour. Matthews went ahead, opening the sliding doors into the kitchen.

"Kana, take Gilmour around the house, lock him in my car and stay with him," Matthews ordered. "O'Flynn, go with him, and once he's secure, bring me back the first aid kit."

Matthews led Vanessa and Lani inside. Mai, in the kitchen as usual, fussed around to mop up the water that dripped off them.

Once they had deposited Kefir on a kitchen chair, the lieutenant cuffed Kefir's hands in front of him.

"What's this for?" he demanded.

"Didn't you hear me? You are under arrest," Matthews said.

Lani grabbed a dish towel and dried her face. "I get big towels," Mai said, and rushed off.

Vanessa took another dish towel to dry her face and neck. She considered trying to dry her hair, but a look at Lani trying that very thing made her decide against it.

Matthews crouched in front of Kefir and tore at the hole in his pants leg made by Gilmour's bullet. He took the dish towel from Vanessa's hand and dabbed at the water and blood, making Kefir flinch and moan. "It's just a superficial wound," he declared. "The bullet made a mess of his pants, but only grazed the skin. You got lucky, son."

"I got shot by your psycho cop!"

"Watch your attitude," the Lieutenant growled. "You'll do a lot better if you cooperate."

Mai ran back in then with a stack of thick, fluffy towels. Gratefully, Vanessa and Lani each took one, patting their clothes as much as they could. Lani started toweling her hair again, while Matthews gently dried Kefir.

O'Flynn returned through the sliding door with the first aid kit. Matthews bandaged Kefir's wound as she took the last towel.

Vanessa dumped his backpack out onto the kitchen table: granola bars, two cans of beer, a plastic bag filled with ground-up, brownish-green leaves, a packet of cigarette rolling papers, a spare t-shirt, now also wet, a folding knife, and a large zip-lock plastic bag of off-white, round pills.

"It looks like he was planning a long absence," Lani said.

"Where is your phone, Kefir?" Vanessa demanded.

"Pocket," he groaned. Vanessa fished it out of the cargo pocket and held it in front of his hands.

"Open it." He touched the screen and it came to life, showing a picture of himself holding a surfboard.

Vanessa opened the phone app. "The last call, less than an hour ago—it's not identified. Who was it from?"

"Josh," Kefir said. "He called me because Gilmour—"

Matthews cut him off. "Remember, everything you say can be used against you," he reminded. He turned to Vanessa. "I've been investigating Gilmour for months. I don't want any reason for this arrest to be thrown out because of a procedural issue."

"Understood, Lieutenant," Vanessa answered.

Janet Sangster came into the kitchen then. "Kefir! Oh my god, what have you done to him?" She tried to run to her boyfriend, but Matthews blocked her.

"I am sorry, Ms. Sangster, but this is a police investigation. You will have to wait outside."

"But he's my boyfriend, and he's injured," she whined.

"He has received first aid, and we are arranging professional medical care as soon as possible," Matthews said, keeping his voice even. "Unfortunately, given the circumstances, that may take some time. But he is in no danger. His injury is superficial."

"Isn't he entitled to a lawyer?" Janet demanded, her voice getting more strident.

Vanessa could see that Matthews was making an effort to be as calming as he could. "Of course. He has not asked for an attorney yet, though."

"I want a lawyer!" Kefir called.

From the pile that had poured out of Kefir's backpack, Vanessa picked up a USB thumb drive. "This is interesting."

"That's my stuff. Keep your paws offa it," Kefir snapped.

"I've already warned you about your attitude," Matthews growled. "You'll get your lawyer. In the meantime, we are cataloging the items found on your person."

"I'll get a lawyer, sweetie!" Janet called and ran down the hallway.

"I can check the contents of the USB drive on Sangster's computer, but I have a feeling I know what's on here," Vanessa said.

"Don't you need a warrant for that?" Kefir said, panic creeping into his voice.

"I can get a warrant by phone in five minutes," Vanessa said to Lani, even though they both knew that a warrant involving a rich celebrity's data would probably take hours to clear.

"I'd like to question him at the station, but we can't get there until someone clears that tree across the road," said Lani.

"Do we need to? We have enough to charge him with all four murders already," Vanessa said.

"Four? What are you talking about? Who else is dead?" Kefir demanded, his eyes darting between Lani and Vanessa. "No way. You can't charge me with murder, not until I get a lawyer."

Lani ignored him. "You're probably right. We have the murder weapons, motive and opportunity," she said, following Vanessa's lead, acting as if they were going to charge Kefir with multiple murders.

"What weapons? I never touched no weapons!" Kefir exclaimed. He started to stand, but collapsed in pain.

"Stay seated," Matthews warned.

"Why don't you save us some time and tell us what's on the thumb drive?" Vanessa said.

Kefir just glared up at her from under his heavy dark brows. "I want a lawyer first."

Someone knocked on the door to the hallway. "I want to speak with my client," said a deep voice.

"Do you have a fairy godmother or something?" Vanessa said.

Alan Guzman, Kathryn's lawyer, stepped into the kitchen, Janet Sangster right behind him. "How long have you been Kefir Steinberg's lawyer?" Lani asked.

"About two minutes. Ms. Sangster—Janet, that is—just hired me to represent Mr. Steinberg. Why have you bound my client?" He stepped close to Kefir, frowning at the mud on his face, arms and clothes and the scratches on his neck from smashing down hemp plants, and of course the blood-soaked pants. "He's injured. He requires medical attention."

"His injuries are superficial, and it's his fault for running and making us tackle him," said Lani.

"He has a wound on his thigh. Why did you chase him?"

"Officer Gilmour went to question him in connection with the death of Josh Fong—"

"Excuse me, who?" the lawyer interrupted.

"The sound engineer. Officer Gilmour told me he was found dead on the Hana Highway."

"I didn't kill him. It was Gilmour!" Kefir yelled.

"Quiet, Steinberg," Vanessa, Lani and Guzman said simultaneously.

"Is this Officer Gilmour?" Guzman asked, nodding toward Lieutenant Matthews.

Matthews pointed to his rank insignia. "I am Lieutenant Matthews, in charge of the Hana station. I have arrested Officer Gilmour for a number of charges, including attempted murder and corruption. Any further information about Officer Gilmour will be forthcoming only after tomorrow."

"How does that have anything to do with my client?" Guzman demanded.

"Gilmour tried to kill me," Kefir whined.

"That is true," Vanessa said.

"You are arresting the victim?"

"I am arresting him for stealing the intellectual property of Steven Sangster, and for trafficking in controlled substances." Vanessa interrupted herself. "By the way, we apprehended him in the middle of his own grow op."

"You don't know that's my weed," said Kefir.

"I have witness testimony to that fact," Vanessa said, leaving out the part that the witness was dead. "But most important, in connection with the death of Isabel West."

"I didn't kill her!" Kefir protested.

"I'd advise you not to speak again until you've been formally charged," said Guzman.

"He's been told his rights. He has legal counsel. He has been given first aid, and it's impossible for anyone to go anywhere for medical care or any other reason right now. So there is no reason Mr. Steinberg cannot answer a few questions."

"Only on my advice," said Guzman, who didn't take his eyes off his client.

Vanessa leaned across the table to look into Kefir's eyes. "Who killed Isabel West?"

Kefir got pale. "I didn't kill nobody."

Matthews pressed the Send button on his radio. "Christine? It's me, Lieutenant Matthews. I'm at the Sangster residence. We will need the van for transporting two suspects, and a CSI team for a crime scene. And talk to the county people to send a crane to move a tree that's blocking the access road." He pressed his finger against the bud in his ear to listen closely. "Yes, we're going to be bringing in at least two suspects for murder. And we're going to need the coroner again—we have another body."

Kefir somehow looked even paler than before. He started shaking. "Who?" he whispered, looking at his lawyer and then at Vanessa. His mouth opened and closed. He jumped to his feet and shouted "I didn't kill Josh! It was that son of a bitch, Gilmour! He called me and told me that Gilmour was running him down."

That's news. "When was this, Mr. Steinberg?" Vanessa asked.

"This morning, after the storm started." Kefir's eyes darted between Vanessa, Lani and his new lawyer. "He told me he was taking the pills off-island. He kept them on his boat. But he phoned me. He said Gilmour was chasing him. I told him to get off the road, but then he screamed and ..." He looked down. Vanessa saw tears trembling at the corners of his eyes. "

Kefir's whole body shook.

"Mr. Steinberg, I must insist that you stop talking right now," Guzman said. He turned to Vanessa. "May I have some time to confer with my client in private?"

"All right," Vanessa agreed. Matthews removed the handcuffs, and Lani led Kefir and Guzman to the closest private area, Sangster's study. Vanessa took the opportunity to retrieve her computer bag.

"And can we get him some dry clothes?" Guzman asked. "He's likely to catch his death in these wet things."

"Hang on, honey, I'll get you some," said Janet, and ran up the stairs.

When only Vanessa, Lani and Matthews remained in the kitchen, Vanessa asked "What have you been investigating Gilmour for?"

"Trafficking in controlled substances," he growled. "Specifically, cody and other opioids. Pills. Hillbilly heroine. And now, we have some solid evidence. I'm hoping to find more."

Vanessa nodded. "That fits what we've found so far."

"You should get out of those wet clothes, yourselves," Matthews said, indicating both Lani and Vanessa.

"I wouldn't mind, but I don't have any clothes here," Lani answered as they returned to the living room.

"I think you look great, all wet like that," said a deep voice. Vanessa and Lani turned to see Perry rising from a chair in a corner of the room, beaming his megawatt smile at them.

"Do you know this man?" Lani asked.

"This is Perry Boyd," Vanessa said, introducing Lani.

"What happened to you?" he asked.

Vanessa was suddenly aware of the mud on her shoes and clothes, and especially the disaster of her hair. "Just a little...mud wrestling."

"You were mud wrestling with someone other

than me?" he joked. He reached out to her face. "Your face is scratched."

"Knock it off, Perry. I am working!"

"What is he doing here?" Lani demanded.

"If he does not stay out of the way, facing a charge of interfering with the course of justice."

"Did I hear you wanted dry clothes?" said a female voice behind them.

They turned to see Kathryn Sangster walking in, carrying an empty wine glass. "I can lend you some, although they may not fit you perfectly."

"Thank you, that would be great," Vanessa said. They followed the widow to one of the many guest rooms, emerging a few minutes later in sweatpants and loose t-shirts.

"At least, they're dry," Lani said.

Vanessa only grunted as she adjusted the shoulder holster for her Walther.

Chapter 16:
The USB

Vanessa and Lani returned to the living room to see most of the household gathered, arguing and questioning about the arrest of Kefir and what it meant. As she came in, they all turned to Vanessa.

The questions rushed at Vanessa like the surf smashing onto a reef. "What's going on? Why are you arresting Kefir? Did he kill Isabel?"

Only Perry remained calm. He sat on a comfortable chair, looking at her with what seemed to be admiration.

"Please, we'll explain everything as soon as possible," she said over and over. "Let the crime scene technicians do their work."

"Another crime scene? Where?" Jeffrey demanded. Paula surprised Vanessa by putting her hand on her husband's arm, trying to calm him.

They all went quiet as they saw the coroner's truck stop behind the fallen koa tree on the road.

Vanessa recognized the tall form of Reid, the CSI chief, followed by his assistant, Sheree Patel. They both wore heavy-duty rain gear, as did two more men carrying a stretcher and a body bag.

Officer O'Flynn took them through the house, to Kaholo Iolani's apartment.

Vanessa hustled out to the covered walkway. When she asked John Reid for a word, she felt decidedly underdressed in a Steven Sangster Revival Tour t-shirt and sweatpants with "Property of Steve" written across her ass. "We have a full search warrant, allowing us to look across the entire compound. Every building, inside and out."

"Okay," Reid said.

"That's what we were intending to do, anyway," Sheree Patel added.

"Good. Once you're finished with Kaholo Iolani's apartment, make your next priority the room where Jeffrey and Paula Sangster are staying. Officer O'Flynn can show you the way. Then, I need another careful, thorough sweep of the studio. Look for opioids."

She went to the games room and plugged the thumb drive into her laptop. Waiting for it to open up, she tried to check her messages.

Nope. Internet is down. Which I figured, in these conditions.

More bad news. The USB key is password protected.

She tried a few obvious guesses, then took out the enigmatic list from Sangster's handwritten note. None worked.

Guess it's time to ask for help. I just wish it was from someone I haven't slept with.

She returned to the living room, where the Sangsters had calmed a little, but conversation still buzzed. Only Perry appeared calm, sitting in a chair in the corner, watching the others.

She leaned close so no one else would hear. "Can you hack into a protected USB drive?" God, he smells good.

Knock it off, Vanessa.

"Do you even need to ask?" Somehow, even more smug.

Vanessa handed him her laptop from her bag, and the USB drive she had taken from Kefir Steinberg's backpack. She watched Perry's fingers move confidently over the keyboard.

He frowned at the screen.

"Hmm. I'm going to need a program I wrote. Fortunately, I always carry it with me. Well, in my bag, actually, which I left in the car. BRB."

He ran out, into the rain. Vanessa watched through the front window as he opened the trunk of his rental car, pulled out a small suitcase, and ran back to the verandah. Even though he had only been in the rain for a minute, he was soaked, dripping onto the floor. Mai showed up with a towel.

Perry pulled his shirt over his head, and Vanessa could not help admiring his chest again. He's still working out.

Then she thought of Perry's naked chest, and the rest of his naked body, under the naked body of her best friend.

Concentrate on the present, Vanessa.

Thanking Mai, Perry toweled off. From his suitcase, he pulled another shirt and a laptop computer bag. After putting on the dry shirt, he took the USB drive out of Vanessa's laptop, plugged it into his own, and settled onto the chair again.

"Give me a few minutes," he said.

Guzman picked that moment to emerge from Sangster's study. "My client would like to make a statement."

Lani and Vanessa followed him into Steven Sangster's office.

Chapter 17:
Kefir talks

Looking at Lani's wild curls, borrowed Lululemon yoga pants and Nickelback t-shirt, Vanessa began to feel a little better about her own appearance.

Through the window, they could see the rain end as quickly as it had begun. The day grew brighter as the clouds moved away from Hana. Birds sang in the trees.

Kefir slumped in clean, dry clothes on the sofa, looking angry. He glared at them defiantly. Guzman sat in a guest chair, scribbling in a little notebook.

"My client is willing to cooperate in return for a plea deal," said the lawyer.

"What kind of deal?" Lani said.

"Drop the murder charges."

"I didn't kill Isabel," Kefir said.

"If that's true, then you have nothing to worry about. But then, why were you running?"

"Do we have an understanding?" Guzman repeated. He held up his smartphone. "I'm recording this, by the way."

"Good," said Lani. She took out her own phone

and activated the recording app. "I guess this is as formal as we can manage in the circumstances. Let's hear some of what he has to offer, and then we'll think about a deal."

With Lani leading this phase of the questioning, Vanessa opened up Steven Sangster's computer again. She scanned through the list of files listed on the letter he had given her through Sophia Keahi, but there was another on the root drive that did not match anything he had written down. She tried opening it, only to be asked for a password.

"Where was Josh going?" Lani asked.

"Up the coast, to Nahiku," he answered.

Vanessa tried the passwords from Sangster's list, but none of them worked.

Lani frowned, bewildered. "Why? It's even smaller than Hana."

"I got a buddy there. Josh and me couldda stayed there till the storm's over. From there, we were gonna get to Kahului, then Honolulu."

"Okay. Why?" Lani asked.

Vanessa spoke up. "Because you were going to sell Steven Sangster's last songs, weren't you? To whom—a publisher for a huge sum, or to some hack singer who'd be willing to pass them off as his own?"

"It was Josh's idea," Kefir said, looking at the floor. "Steve wanted to record these songs with Erica Harrison. He thought it would be a comeback for both of them. Josh said these songs were the best Steve wrote in years."

"Are these different from the songs that his wife will record?" Lani asked.

Kefir barked a laugh. "Those songs Kathryn's working on? Have you heard them?" He shook his head. "Josh played them for me one day. They're crap. That's Steve writing 'New Country,' tryin' to sound like Luke Bryan or Keith Urban. They're not Steven Sangster songs."

"Why did he do that?" Vanessa asked.

"'Cuz that's what Kathryn wants. She thinks she's the next Carrie Underwood. And sometimes, the next Beyoncé, too. But she's awful. And no matter how good a producer Josh is and how much he bangs her, he's never gonna make her a good singer."

"So you are confirming that Josh was sleeping with Kathryn Sangster?" Lani asked.

"Oh, yeah. Everyone knew it. Even Steven. But he was bangin' Isabel, so he didn't much care. And he knew how bad a singer Kathryn is, too. That's why he was writin' new songs in his own style and planning to record 'em with Erica Harrison."

"Did Kathryn know that Steven did not like her singing?"

Kefir shrugged. "Prob'ly not. She never really cared about Steve's music. She liked his money and her fantasy about marryin' a big star and him makin' *her* a big star."

"I don't get it—Josh was working with Steven on the recording," Vanessa asked. "If these songs really are that good and will sell so well, wouldn't he make more money from being the producer of a new Steven Sangster and Erica Harrison album, than whatever some hack songwriter can pay you?"

"Josh didn't come up with that scheme until after Steve died. The songs aren't finished, yet. That's why Erica came. But with Steve dead, they're worthless unless another musician can finish what Steve started."

The computer screen and the lights flickered, then got brighter. They were all aware again of the sound of the generator, which had been humming low in the background somewhere, running down. "Looks like the power's back," said Lani.

Vanessa picked up the phone on Sangster's desk and heard a dial tone. She put it back down and came around the desk to look down at Kefir.

"What is the password to open the files on the USB we found in your backpack?" Vanessa asked.

Kefir gave her a completely blank expression. "Josh didn't tell me there was a password."

"Why did you kill Isabel West, Kefir?" Lani asked.

"Hold on there, Special Agent," said Guzman. "You have not actually charged my client yet, nor have you disclosed any evidence about that circumstance. And remember the plea deal? Mr. Steinberg has answered many of your questions, but before he goes any further, he will only speak in return for not being charged with any homicides or anything other than resisting arrest."

"We will have to confer with the District Attorney about that," said Vanessa. "Tell me, Kefir, what was your cut from the sale of the songs?"

"I will have to stop this interview now," Guzman interrupted again. "My client and I need to confer for a few more minutes."

"That's fine," Vanessa said. "I have another line of enquiry to pursue."

She picked up Sangster's computer, and with Lani, left the office.

Time to see what Perry has found.

Chapter 18:
Songs of Steven Sangster

Lani trailing, Vanessa went looking for her...*boyfriend? Former boyfriend? Stalker?* Most of the household, including Kathryn, Jeffrey and Paula Sangster and their daughters, and even Mai, the cook, had gathered in the kitchen where Mai was serving tea, coffee and snacks. Probably to get whatever news they could. Perry sat on a high stool near the counter, chatting with Paula.

"Well? Any results?" Vanessa demanded.

Perry gave Paula a hint of his floodlight smile, then turned the full effect on Vanessa. "Wow. You look so cute in those clothes."

Does he have to do this with Lani right here? "The USB," Vanessa growled. "Kefir does not know the password."

Perry scoffed as he flipped his laptop open on the coffee table in front of him. "Like *I* need a password."

Vanessa leaned over his shoulder to look at the screen. She could smell him again, bringing back memories of delicious sensuality. She pushed them away. *Concentrate.* "Come with me," she said, and led him to the games room.

They sat, close together on a leather sofa. Vanessa was careful not to let her leg touch his, but their shoulders came together. She was conscious that Lani had not followed them.

Perry pointed at the screen of his laptop. "That window is the contents of the USB drive."

Vanessa's eyes ran down the list of file names. Some were text files, but others had a sound icon with names like "You Are My Ocean," "Home," "Rock Shore" and "Open my Heart."

Steven Sangster's new songs. His last ones. "Can you open them?" Vanessa asked.

Perry double-clicked one of the sound icons. Within seconds, they heard the distinct sound of Steven Sangster strumming a guitar, then his gravelly, honest voice.

"He sounds weaker than he used to, but this is good," Perry said. "Not really my style, but good."

"This is the best I've heard from Steven Sangster in years," Vanessa agreed. "It's a lot better than the song I heard Kathryn sing yesterday."

"Who's Kathryn?"

"His new trophy wife. Or rather, the new widow. Steven Sangster wrote some songs for her, and she's laboring under the delusion that his material will make her a star."

"Well, there's no shortage of country stars with

bad voices," Perry said, looking at her in that way she had always found so … irresistible.

Concentrate on the job, she told herself again. "Thank you, Perry," she said. "Is this unlocked now?"

"Give me a sec," he replied, and he finger-danced on the keyboard again. "There. Password protection removed. You have a completely open thumb drive to play with." He stood, making a grand gesture of giving Vanessa the USB stick.

"Great." She handed him Sangster's laptop. "There's one folder there that I cannot open. Labelled 'Investigate.' It wants a password that I don't have. See if you can open it."

Perry beamed again. "Piece of cake."

They returned to the study. Lani sat facing Kefir while Vanessa went behind the desk and opened Sangster's computer.

"So, you and Josh Fong. Which one of you killed Kaholo Iolani?" Lani asked.

Kefir's head snapped back up. "Kaholo?" He looked at his lawyer. "Kaholo is dead? When? How? Oh my god. Neither of us would kill Kaholo. I liked him!"

"When did you last see Fong, Kefir?"

"This morning, after we found Isabel—I mean, after everybody else found out about Isabel. I didn't hear anything about Kaholo until you mentioned it, just now. What happened to him?"

"Detective Ferreira, what does this have to do

with the charges—if any—facing my client?"

"We haven't charged him, yet," Lani retorted. "We're not able to get to the station."

"Exactly my point, Detective. Introducing new lines of questioning is not appropriate at this point. Furthermore," he turned to Kefir, "my client is not obligated, nor is he advised, to answer questions until we know what the charges are, and what evidence there may be."

"Evidence includes a multi-acre field of hemp, quantities of marijuana, and enough of a controlled substance to put your client behind bars for several years."

"What controlled substances?"

"Oxycodone."

"That wasn't my idea. That was Josh's," Kefir protested.

"Mr. Steinberg, please do not say anymore until the police formally charge you," Guzman warned.

"I didn't want to get involved in the cody. It was all Josh's idea. The pills, the music…"

"Kefir, shut up, will you?" Guzman shouted.

"I told Josh to forget the cody. Just to ditch it. Let Gilmour have the pills and the money, but he decided to run. He was going to Nahiku. I said he should wait, but he wanted to get the rest of the cody and the music files and get to California as soon as—"

"My last warning before I resign your case, Mr.

Steinberg. *Shut up!*" said Guzman.

A knock on the door preceded its opening. Matthews poked his head in. "The town crew has arrived to move the tree. We can take the suspects to the station."

"Good," Vanessa said. "I think we have enough here."

Lani snapped handcuffs on Kefir again as Janet ran into the room. "What are you doing?"

"Please stand aside, Ms. Sangster," Lani said, pushing Kefir toward the door. "We are taking Mr. Steinberg to be processed and charged as an accessory to murder, fraud and theft."

"Guzman, you're his lawyer," Janet cried, chasing them into the living room. "Stop this!"

"I resign. I cannot represent a client who will not stop talking when I tell him to shut up. Besides, it's a conflict of interest with my existing relationship, representing Mrs. Kathryn Sangster." He went to Kathryn, who stood beside the grand piano, and took her hand between both of his. "Mrs. Sangster, I advise you not to say another word until we've had a complete conference." Kathryn nodded dumbly, looking more shocked than anyone else in the room.

Outside, four men in hard hats and reflective vests watched a truck with County of Maui markings winch the fallen koa tree out of the way.

Matthews got into his Maui PD SUV, with Kana and the handcuffed Gilmour in the back seat. O'Flynn held the door as Lani put the handcuffed

Kefir Steinberg in the back of Lani's vehicle, then climbed in beside him.

"Coming with us to the station?" Lani asked Vanessa.

"Wouldn't miss it for the world." Vanessa glanced over her shoulder, but saw no sign of the CSI team.

She had no doubt they'd come to her soon.

Chapter 19:
Interviews

On the short ride to the Hana police substation, Vanessa opened the once-locked "Investigate" folder on Sangster's laptop. A quick scan told her she had guessed right about its contents.

Got you.

At the station, she nodded a greeting to Christine Nolfi, the receptionist she had met on her previous visit to Hana. She admired Matthews' experienced efficiency as he processed Gilmour, then Steinberg, fingerprinting them, taking their potentially dangerous personal belongings and photographing them.

She picked up Steinberg's cell phone. "Unlock it."

"Why?"

"I want to verify some information on it that would be good for you." At his puzzled expression, she added, "Your last incoming call from Josh Fong." He tapped four times on the screen, and it came to life.

Matthews put Kefir into a small lockup cage, and then led Gilmour to the station's sole interview room. After handcuffing the disgraced officer to the little metal table in the middle of the room, he came out again and fetched a cloth bag from the front entrance.

"I've been investigating Gilmour for close to a year," he said to Vanessa and Lani. "And now, thanks to you two, I got him."

"For what?"

"Corruption, for a start. But mostly, trafficking in opioids all over this part of Maui."

"So, Kefir was not lying," Vanessa said.

"Oh, I'm sure he was lying," Matthews said. "Just not about that one particular item."

"Why were you investigating him? Gilmour, I mean."

"There were hints, little clues that he was dirty. Officer O'Flynn started watching him like a hawk about six months ago. She and I collected some corroborating evidence, but we wanted to find his connections. Now, it seems to have been Fong."

"His name wasn't Fong," Vanessa said. "It was Lanh Ngo. He was a Vietnamese national, and probably an illegal alien, as well."

Matthews nodded. "Makes sense."

"When did you plan on informing me about this?" Lani asked.

"Sorry. I just found out this morning when Mai Pham, the cook, told me. I have a feeling we'll find he has a pretty extensive record, too. But I have to ask you, Lieutenant Matthews—what was Fong doing out on the road in the storm?" Vanessa asked.

"I think he was trying to run, but Gilmour found him," Matthews answered. "The way I see it, Gilmour chased Josh Fong until Fong crashed his car in Hana, then ran him down when Fong tried to flee on foot. He called it in as an accident, and I went there, along with the coroner to collect the body."

Vanessa held up Fong's cell phone. "I have something that will confirm that. The last incoming call to Kefir's phone was from Fong-Ngo. Kefir said that Josh had called him, saying that Gilmour was trying to run him down."

"He didn't want new competition," Matthews said. "When I got back to the station with Fong's body, Gilmour did not show up, like he should have. That told me things were coming to a head. Gilmour was going to make his move," said Matthews. "My move was to go to the Sangster place."

"Just in time, too," said Lani.

"That gave me the final piece of evidence we all need to tie this case up," Matthews added. He opened the door. "Want to sit in?"

Gilmour, still in uniform but without a belt, shoes or any police equipment, looked uncomfortable, sitting on a little metal chair with his hands handcuffed to a metal bar bolted to the table in front of him. He glared defiantly at Vanessa and

Lani.

Matthews opened the door again at a single knock. In came a young woman with thick, short black hair, light brown skin and black rimmed glasses. She wore a light blue blazer over what Vanessa thought was a far too casual summer dress.

"Juana Estrella, public defender," said Matthews. "These are FBI Special Agent Vanessa Storm, and I think you know Detective Sergeant Ferreira from Kahului."

Estrella rose and shook their hands, then sat beside her client.

Vanessa and Lani sat in two uncomfortable chairs next to the door as Matthews turned on a video camera set up on a tripod in the corner.

Vanessa's tablet computer chirped. She swiped her finger across the screen and opened the secure messaging app. With the storm over, it looked like full Internet access was back in service.

She brought up the latest email from King. The attachments seemed to have everything she had asked for. *It's amazing when you realize how dependent you are on the Internet when it goes down for a couple of hours.*

Matthews sat down across the table from Estrella and Gilmour, and recited the date, place, and the names of those in the room.

"Samuel Gilmour, you have been read your civil rights and charged with attempted murder, obstruction of justice, violation of the public trust, and possession of controlled substances for the purpose of trafficking."

"What controlled substances?" Gilmour demanded.

Matthews dumped the contents of the cloth bag onto the table: three large, clear plastic bags filled with whitish round pills. "We found these in your car. There's enough here on their own to convict you."

Estrella began scribbling in a lined notebook.

"Those are not mine," Gilmour said.

"No. They were Lanh Ngo's."

Gilmour frowned. "Who?"

"A man you know as Josh Fong. You took these from him after you ran him down. But you didn't have time to stash them anywhere but your car before you had to go back to the Sangster place and take care of the last loose end, did you? That loose end being Kefir Steinberg."

"Those pills were evidence that I took from Fong. Or Ngo, or whatever you want to call him."

"You went immediately from Ngo's body to kill Kefir Steinberg."

"Do you have evidence of that, Lieutenant?" Estrella asked.

"We have Officer Gilmour's sidearm, which is awaiting analysis by our CSI, and we have eyewitness accounts of Agent Storm and Detective Ferreira, here." Matthews nodded to the two by the door. "Not to mention, the attempted murder victim, himself."

"I thought he was going to fire a gun," Gilmour argued.

"He did not even have a cell phone in his hands," said Matthews. "With the training you received, you know you had no justification for drawing your weapon on an unarmed man who was running away from you. Not to mention that you endangered three other officers around the victim."

"I've already told you, Lieutenant. I took those pills from Fong's vehicle, and then I went to find his accomplice at the Sangster house. Then I was told to arrest Steinberg, by her." He pointed his chin toward Vanessa. "He ran right away, and I chased him. Maybe I was wrong to shoot when I did, but like I said, I thought he was armed. That was a perfectly reasonable assumption." His tone changed, softened. He leaned forward and tried to look Matthews in the eye. "You got it all wrong, Lieutenant. I was in the middle of taking down a drug dealer, and you arrest *me*."

Matthews returned the suspect's gaze. He pushed the pills aside and centered his tablet computer on the table, tapping on the screen. Photos opened, and Matthews slowly swiped through a series. "We've been watching you for months, Gilmour. We have a lot more evidence. For example, here you are, out of uniform, with Ngo." He swiped to another photo. "You in Nahiku with known drug dealers." He swiped again. "Your storage locker in Hana, which is full of opioid trace."

"I have never seen that locker before, and I don't have a storage locker, anywhere."

Matthews sighed. "You didn't rent it in your own name, but we've definitely tied it to you. We have more, as well."

Estrella cut in. "My client has nothing more to say until we have an opportunity to review all the other evidence. Which, at this point, appears completely circumstantial."

Matthews stood, gathering the pills and tablet computer. "Yes. You'll get full discovery, which I anticipate will be after Officer Gilmour is transferred to court lockup in Kahului."

He turned off the video camera and held the door open for Lani and Vanessa. "Thank you, officers. I hope this sheds some light on your investigation."

After taking Gilmour to the lockup cage, Matthews led Steinberg to the interview room. Estrella and Vanessa followed them. Vanessa sat down to lead the questions.

She read the date and names for the video record, then looked closely at Kefir.

"Now, Kefir, we have talked already about the music, about Josh and Isabel. You have given us a lot of information already, but now I want you to tell us everything you can about the opioids. The pills," she added for clarity.

"What about my deal?" Kefir demanded.

"Please, hold on, Agent Storm," Estrella interrupted. "I have not had a minute to come up to speed on this case. Was there a plea bargain?"

"No agreement was made, Ms. Estrella, although Mr. Steinberg did ask for one. I said any information he could share would be taken into account by the District Attorney, but he volunteered a good deal of information with that understanding."

"I understood I'd get a deal," Kefir protested.

"No one agreed to that," Vanessa retorted. To Estrella, she said "We can give you copies of audio recordings of the interviews."

"I will need those. Go ahead with the interview, but I warn you, that if anything abrogates Mr. Steinberg's interests, I will end this procedure."

Vanessa nodded at that. "Now, Kefir, tell us about the pills. You said it was Fong's idea. Remember, you have already admitted to knowing about them."

Kefir looked to his appointed lawyer, who nodded. "Yeah, I knew about them. I didn't want to get into pills, but Josh said we could make a lot of money with them. I wanted to stick to selling weed—"

"Wait," Estrella interrupted again. "You have just incriminated yourself."

"Not really," Vanessa said. "We have a number of witnesses who have stated that." *Although they're dead.*

"That's all right," said Kefir. "Everybody knows I planted that weed. But it was for Steven."

"Steven?" the lawyer asked.

"Sangster. You know—"

"The singer. Yes, I know. A tragic loss." Her face did not betray any emotion.

"The marijuana is not an issue at this point," Vanessa said. "The point of this enquiry is to determine how Steven Sangster died, and who shot at his son, Jeffrey, Detective Ferreira and me, and the circumstances around the deaths of Isabel West and Kaholo Iolani. And to find out about the distribution of illegal opioids through the Sangster property."

"I told you, that was Josh's idea!" Kefir repeated.

Vanessa nodded. "Duly noted. What was Josh's source?"

Kefir glanced again at his lawyer, but she remained impassive. "Well ... at first, it was Gilmour, the cop."

Vanessa heard Matthews shuffle his feet behind her. *That's what he needed.*

"Gilmour was the source. I don't know where he got them from, but he was the big distributor around here. Actually, probably half of Maui. I don't know. Josh became a big dealer. He kept the pills in his boat, so he could ditch them if he had to. And he pressured me to sell them—"

"Stop right there, Mr. Steinberg," Estrella said.

"—but then, he said he found a new source. Someone direct from overseas. China, Taiwan, maybe Thailand, I don't know—"

"Mr. Steinberg, it's my understanding that you have already had an attorney resign your case because you refused to stop talking. As I am the only public defender currently in Hana, I suggest you stop talking before I follow Mr. Guzman's example."

Kefir swallowed. "All I said was 'he pressured me.' I didn't say I actually did it."

"What do you know about Josh Fong, Kefir?" Vanessa asked.

Kefir shrugged. "He showed up a coupla months ago, to record Steve's music—"

"Steve Sangster was recording again?" Estrella said, unable to hide the excitement in her voice.

"Uh, yeah, and Josh was a sound engineer."

"What else do you know about him, Kefir?" asked Vanessa.

"Uh, I think he's—he was from California. L.A., I think."

"Have you heard the name 'Lahn Ngo'?" Kefir's face was blank. "That was his real name. He was from Vietnam." She pushed her tablet across the table for Kefir to see.

"According to the State Department, Ngo had a long criminal record in Ho Chi Minh City. He was convicted five years ago in California for assault and battery and spent nine months in a federal correctional facility, where apparently he learned enough to pass himself off as a qualified sound engineer."

All the color drained out of Kefir's face. "I had no idea," he whispered.

"I'm going to need to see that," said Estrella.

"You'll get it in discovery," Vanessa said. "Tell us, Kefir, who was Ngo going to sell the new Steven Sangster songs to?"

"No comment," Estrella said. "You have not established that my client had anything to do with that."

"Fine. Why don't you tell us why he killed Isabel West?"

"Don't answer that," said the lawyer. Kefir swallowed.

"Then tell us how you found the gun that shot at us yesterday—at Sergeant Ferreira, Jeffrey Sangster and me?"

"Wait—this is a charge I am not familiar with," Estrella began.

"Mr. Steinberg presented that gun to me earlier today." She swiped her tablet's screen until it showed the picture she had taken of it. "He took it out of a bag under his jacket and put it in my hands. So how did you find it, Kefir?"

Kefir's eyes darted around the little room. "It was Josh—or Ngo, or whoever. He told me I would find the gun that shot at you yesterday in the garden shed under Kaholo's apartment."

"How did he know about it?"

"I don't wanna—oh, well, they're both dead, now. It won't make any difference. Josh said he saw Kaholo yesterday morning, standing on the walkway outside his apartment, firing that big honkin' gun. I didn't wanna get Kaholo in trouble, but Josh said ... he said it was him or me."

"Either you or he would get the gun?"

"No, well, yes, but mostly, if we didn't give up Kaholo, the cops were gonna get *us*. They'd—you'd find the pills, and the weed, and the music, and then it would all be over."

"So you gave up Kaholo Iolani as the shooter, to protect yourself?"

Kefir nodded. A tear slid down his cheek.

"I think we should stop there," Estrella said. "Mr. Steinberg has volunteered a great deal of information. Before this goes on, I think some consideration is in order."

"Consideration?"

"A plea bargain. A reduction in charges in return for further information."

"That cannot happen until the district attorney has a chance to review the information," Matthews interjected. "And given the hour and the fact that the nearest DA is in Paia, that won't be before tomorrow."

"Then I guess we're done until tomorrow," Estrella said, closing her notebook.

"Wait—does that mean I gotta stay here overnight?" Kefir began to tremble.

"Don't worry," Matthews said. "We won't leave you in the same cage as Gilmour." Matthews opened the door to let in Officer Kana, who unlocked Kefir's handcuffs and led him away.

"I wouldn't worry too much about Kefir's feelings," Vanessa told Matthews. "He stood by and watched as Ngo put a plastic bag over Isabel's head and suffocated her to death."

John Reid and Sheree Patel came into the station as Vanessa and Lani stepped out of the interview room. Reid's face lit up. "You were right on the money. We got trace in Paula Sangster's suitcases."

"What kind of trace?"

"Narcotics. Opiate of some kind. We'll have to analyze it in the lab, but I'll bet it will match the narcotic trace we got from Kaholo Iolani's quarters, and the residue in the syringe by his body."

"Don't forget the blood," said Sheree Patel. "Droplets on the sleeve of one of her blouses. *I'll* bet it matches Iolani's, as well. *And* black hair. That will also require lab analysis, but to me, it looked a lot like Iolani's."

Reid nodded.

Vanessa's phone chimed. It was a text from Alan Terakawa, her FBI partner. *Just landed Hana airpt. Pol stn in 10.* She tapped out a quick reply. *Meet me at Sangster rez.*

"Thanks," she said to the CSI team. "Send me your reports as soon as you can." To Matthews, she asked "Is Officer O'Flynn still at the Sangster house?" Matthews nodded.

Vanessa turned to Lani. "Give me a lift back there?"

Chapter 20:
Clearing up

The drive to the Sangster estate took only minutes in the clear, soft light of early evening, but Vanessa was in no hurry. Her quarry was not about to go anywhere.

As Lani drove up to the access road to the estate, the coroner's wagon passed them, headed back to the village. Lani parked the SUV between two Maui PD SUVs and passed three CSI techs coming out the front door.

Lani held Vanessa back on the front steps. "I've waited long enough for your surprise. Why are we here?"

"To arrest the killer of Kaholo Iolani. But first, give me a few minutes. I want to get the little girls out of the way. Watch for my signal."

Inside the big house, Officer O'Flynn was still in the living room, looking embarrassed to see Janet and Jeffrey screaming at each other. They broke off, both in mid-sentence, when Vanessa came in. "Officer O'Flynn, can you gather the rest of the family here?"

"Why?" Jeffrey asked.

"I have to talk to you all about Kaholo Iolani's

murder," Vanessa said.

Janet cried out, but Jeffrey looked confused. "I thought he overdosed," he said.

"He did, but not alone. Please, Mr. Sangster, come into the study with me for a moment."

She shut the study door behind them and pulled the small, clear plastic evidence bag from her pocket. "Do you recognize this, Mr. Sangster?"

He bent closer, squinting. He took a corner of the bag between thumb and finger and lifted it, but Vanessa kept a hold on the top. "Yes, I do. It's an earring I bought my wife last year. Why do you have it?" He suddenly looked her in the eye, his breath caught in his throat. "What are you saying?"

Vanessa opened the door in time to see O'Flynn and Lani stepping into the living room behind Mai. The rest of the household were all gathered in the room, much like they had been the day earlier: Janet and her children, Ben and Madison; Paula Sangster, scowling on a sofa with her three scared looking daughters; Kathryn Sangster slumping on an easy chair, a glass of wine in her hand; and Erica Harrison standing beside the piano.

There were important differences, though. Perry was hanging around, Kefir Steinberg was in the lockup in Hana, while Isabel West, Josh Fong—or Lanh Ngo—and Kaholo Iolani were dead.

Out the window, Vanessa could see another police cruiser pulling up. It came to the bottom of the steps, and when the door opened, she saw Alan Terakawa climb out of the passenger side. He ran up the steps like a pouncing leopard, sprang into the house, and showed O'Flynn his Bureau ID.

"Paula, would you come over here, please?" Vanessa called.

"No!" Jeffrey yelled, even as his wife stood. She looked worried, and paused to pat her girls reassuringly. "How dare you—"

Vanessa pushed Jeffrey into the study. "Do you really want to make this scene in front of your daughters, Mr. Sangster?"

Paula came into the study, with Terakawa behind her. He shut the door and stood in front of it. Paula noticed and for the first time, looked scared.

Vanessa showed her the earring. "Recognize this?"

"My earring," she said with forced enthusiasm. "I have been looking for it. Where did you find it?"

"First, why don't you tell me what you know about Kaholo Iolani."

"Don't answer that, honey," Jeffrey said. "Not without a lawyer."

Paula's eyes flashed with anger, then clouded with worry. "What do I need a lawyer for, sweetie? Because of my earring?" She turned to Vanessa. "Are you saying that Kaholo stole my diamond earring?"

"Why would he do that, Mrs. Sangster?" said

Vanessa.

"What else? To support his drug habit, of course." She leaned closer and her voice dropped to a hoarse whisper. "You know, he was a heroin addict."

"How do you know that?" Vanessa asked.

"Everyone knew that," Paula answered. Her slight Spanish accent deepened, as did the color on her face. "And every time we come here, I have to worry about my little girls being exposed to that kind of degeneracy. But Steven, he didn't care," she hissed.

"Paula, shut up!" her husband yelled.

She turned to him. "Don't you tell me to shut up, you weakling. You could have had everything, this estate, the money, the music rights, *everything*, if you had the balls to do what I told you to do years ago."

"Paula, this is not the time or place—"

"No, *you* shut up. You're not as smart as you think you are, and now you've ruined everything. You lost your father's money and now to make up for that, you kill him!"

"Paula!" Jeffrey stepped back from his wife, shaking, his eyes wide. "No, I didn't —"

Paula shrieked, her face red, spit flying from her lips. "That's why Kaholo tried to shoot you. You killed his friend, you imbecile."

"No, Paula, no, I would never ..."

Paula stepped toward her husband, her hand

raised for a slap, but Vanessa caught her wrist, and twisted her arm behind her back. "That's enough, Mrs. Sangster. Your husband did not kill his father, at least not directly. Steven Sangster died of a heart attack."

"He brought it on," Paula snarled. "Arguing with him at night. I know what happened. He got the old man so worked up his heart gave out."

Vanessa looked at Jeffrey. He hung his head, looking at something fascinating on the floor. "It's true," he said. "We argued. I shouldn't have been so ... so strident. So stubborn. But so was he!"

Vanessa pushed Paula to sit on a sofa. "What happened that night, Jeffrey?"

Jeffrey drew a deep breath, then let the whole story out at once. He surprised Vanessa with a vivid description that made her feel like she had been there, two nights previously.

Stars fill the sky above as two men walk across the grounds of the dark Sangster house. They talk, first in low tones, gradually getting louder as they get farther from the group of buildings.

"I got big plans for this new album," says the taller man."

Vanessa could picture him, his grey hair still thick, with the wave over his ears, curling up just above his shoulders. His short grey beard, the laugh lines around his piercing blue eyes. "I have found new inspiration. It's going to be my swan song. Face it, son, I don't have that many good years left."

"Don't say that, Pop," says the younger man. Shorter than his father, he also has not inherited the long legs, wide shoulders nor the classic good looks. And unlike the rangy, still fit father, the son is shorter with a slouch and potbelly. "But a new album will cost money to produce. Don't forget the expense. You really can't afford it."

"You have to spend money to make money," says Steve Sangster in his trademark growl. He continues leading his son across the grounds to where the rain forest looms in the night like a black wall.

They continue onto a narrow path, water dripping onto them from the leaves above. "You've already spent a fortune on new equipment. All that high-tech stuff—you never used that before. You used to make music with just an acoustic guitar and a single microphone."

"Keep up, son!" says Steve Sangster. "No serious musician in the world does that, anymore. I haven't for forty years! No, high tech is where recording is at, these days. It doesn't change the music—it *enhances* it."

"It's expensive. And speaking of expensive, what you're paying that producer is ridiculous."

"If you mean Josh Fong, his rates are actually pretty reasonable."

"What about room and board? Christ, Pop, you've practically *adopted* him."

"Is that what this is about? Are you jealous

because you think you've got a new brother or something?" The elder Sangster barks a laugh.

"Of course not. I'm just talking about the expense."

They step out from under the rain forest canopy, onto the lava floor of the ruined heiau. Steven stops and looks up to admire the stars. "Careful," he says as his son joins him on the platform. "There's a pretty wicked drop-off on the other side."

"I remember," says the younger Sangster.

Steve sighs. "This is going to be my last comeback, son. I have a lot of ideas. Good ideas. I've sent samples to Erica, and she agrees. She's coming tomorrow to collaborate on finishing the songs and record them with me."

"Erica? Harrison?"

Steve brings his intense glare on his son. "Yes. My ex-wife. The country singing star. She still has a big fan base."

"So, you're going to record a duet album," Jeffrey whines. "Which means you'll have to divide the receipts with her. Which means even less income. Tell me, is she going to contribute to the costs, too?"

"Will you shut up about the money?" Steven cries. "This album is going to be a hit, I tell you. They're good songs. Good music, and Erica is going to help make them as good as they can be. The sales are going to make the production costs look like nothing."

It is Jeffrey's turn to sigh. "Pop, you're dreaming. I'm sorry, but have you looked at your numbers lately? Your last three albums all lost money. You haven't performed on a stage in how long now?"

"Are you sayin' you don't believe in your old man?" Steve growls.

"I'm saying it's a huge risk. The costs could far exceed any sales. They almost certainly will, especially considering the promotion you're talking about. A tour, advertising, the whole thing."

"You don't believe in me."

"I believe in you. You're a great musician, Pop! But the music industry has moved on. I'm sorry, but you just don't have the audience numbers anymore."

"That's a really shitty thing to say."

"Pop, I'm just trying to look out for your interests."

Steve laughs, loud and bitter. "*My* interests? You dare say that after you show me those papers you wanted me to sign? The documents that give you more control over my money?"

"I need your authorization to sell some bonds to cover previous losses."

"Those losses are your fault," Steve says, his voice rising. "*You* made those decisions."

"Yes, I have made some mistakes."

"I notice that you still managed to maintain your own lifestyle. The cars, the private school, the trips. Christ, how much jewelry does Paula *need*?" Steve yells.

"Pop!" Jeffrey yells back. "Are you accusing me of robbing you?"

"You're just trying to make sure that you inherit as much as possible. Well, forget it. I'm leaving the compound to the Hawaiian cultural society, not to an ungrateful little shit like you."

Jeffrey explodes. "You're a senile, selfish old man! You're still dreaming of being a pop star. Your fawning groupies were always more important to you than your children."

Steve Sangster's response is even more explosive. "And you're a bad son. You're too weak to stand up to your wife and set limits for your kids. You're too timid to step out from behind your goddamned spreadsheets. And you're too much of a coward to do anything but take money from your father!"

"I don't hear you complaining about giving money to your daughter."

"Don't you dare compare yourself to Janet. At least she cares about her father."

"She's just a leech, and you know it."

"You take that back!" Steve screamed.

"No. She's a leech, and you're a ... *a bad father*."

"You little prick!" Steve lurches toward his son, stumbles and lets out a strangled gurgle. His hand goes to his chest. He leans to one side, and then disappears.

"Pop!" Jeffrey cries. He steps to the edge, peering down. He fumbles in his pants until he pulls his phone out of his pocket. He shines its light down into the fissure beside the heiau. "Oh, Pop."

Trembling, he sits on the edge of the hole in the ground, then slides down to the bottom. He touches his father gingerly, hesitating. Then he shakes the man a little harder. "Oh, no."

He holds his hand under his father's nose, and feels no breath. He presses two fingers against the man's neck, and finds no pulse.

"Damn it, damn it ..."

Still holding his phone in one hand, he clambers awkwardly out of the hole. He keeps slipping on the wet ground, the light from his phone casting erratic shadows as he climbs. At the heiau, he runs back down the path to the compound.

"Wait a minute," Lani interrupted him. "You told me and the other police officers that you didn't arrive until the next morning."

Jeffrey mumbled like a child. "I lied. I had come that night by myself, just to try to talk some sense into my father."

Vanessa wished she had turned on her recorder, but that would require Mirandizing the Sangsters, which she still planned to do. Still, she had Alan Terakawa as a witness, and if Jeffrey told the story now, he'd probably be more likely to repeat it in court, if needed.

Jeffrey looked at Terakawa, as if another man would be more understanding. Tears streamed down his cheeks. "God, I was awful. I panicked. I thought for sure I'd be blamed for killing him. Because it was my fault, after all. So I ran. I got back into my car. I figured no one had seen me, because I came to the house after dark and Dad opened the door himself."

"Except someone did see you. Kaholo saw you, you idiot," said Paula.

Jeffrey let that one go. "I drove home as fast as I dared, and let me tell you, the Hana Highway is not something you want to drive on in the middle of the night.

"We got the call early the next morning that Dad was dead, and we all jumped in the car and drove back here as fast as we could."

He paused again, looking from Terakawa to Vanessa and back. "So you see, it's really all my fault. My wife had nothing to do with it. Let her go."

Vanessa nodded at Terakawa, who stepped directly behind Jeffrey. "The trouble with that, Jeffrey, is that we have evidence," she said.

"What evidence?"

"Blood droplets, black hair and opiates on Paula Sangster's clothing."

"What? How—"

"Our search warrant covers every inch of the house and the grounds," Vanessa explained. "I directed the crime scene investigators to look especially at your rooms, Mrs. Sangster. And that paid off.

"And the earlier testing confirmed that the slug found on the grounds was indeed fired from the gun that Kefir Steinberg gave us—the antique firearm that Steven Sangster gave Kaholo Iolani from his collection. The CSI team also found gunpowder trace on the railing of the walkway outside Mr. Iolani's apartment."

"What are you saying?" Jeffrey asked, his voice hoarse. But his expression told Vanessa that he already knew.

"Paula Sangster, you are under arrest in relation to the death of Kaholo Iolani."

"That's ridiculous," Jeffrey exclaimed.

Paula looked at Vanessa, then at her husband, and finally covered her face with her hands and sobbed.

"Mrs. Sangster, if you can pull yourself together, I am willing to escort you to a police vehicle without handcuffs, so your daughters don't see you restrained. Can you do that?"

Paula sobbed one more time, then took a deep breath, shook her head and her long brown hair and wiped her face. Her eyes and cheeks were still red, but she seemed to be under control.

Vanessa turned to Jeffrey. "Mr. Sangster, you are under arrest for suspicion of manslaughter, and an indignity on a human body."

Jeffrey turned white. "Wha—what are you

talking about?" he gasped.

"Either you left a dying man without attempting to find help, or you did not report finding a dead person. Either way, they're serious charges. I will also let you leave without handcuffs in front of your children, if you can cooperate."

She stepped behind the Sangsters. "Alan, can you get the door?" Terakawa led the way out of the house, and Vanessa stayed close behind Paula.

"What's going on?" Janet asked, echoed by Kathryn.

"Where are Mommy and Daddy going?" asked the eldest Sangster girl.

"We're just going to the police station to answer some questions. To help the police," said Jeffrey, taking a chance to pull his daughters together into a group hug.

Lani leaned close to O'Flynn. "Call child services."

Chapter 21:
Everything except the paperwork

At the Hana station again, Vanessa found a desk and a printer to make hard copies of all her documentation: warrants, crime scene forensic reports, preliminary findings from the coroner and an unofficial but definitive report on the first death that started this whole case.

She took it to a small conference-cum-lunch room, where Lani had set up a webcam and two monitors for a remote debrief with their respective superiors.

On one monitor was Al King in the Honolulu FBI office. The other screen displayed the broad, brown face of Kaimi Kekoa, who was acting head of detectives at the Kahului office of the Maui PD.

Alan Terakawa and Lani sat at the lunch/conference table, eating huli huli chicken someone had brought in from a local food stand. Vanessa sat down where a third plate had been put for her.

"Looks like you had this pretty well wrapped up before I even took off from Oahu," said

Terakawa. "Hogging all the fun." He dug into a bowl of papaya salad.

"Was it just the earring that made you suspect Paula for killing Kaholo?" Lani asked around a mouthful.

Vanessa picked up a drumstick. She had never had so little time to eat or look after herself as on this case, surrounded by rich rock stars.

"Let me get this straight," said King through the monitor. "Paula Sangster, the singer's daughter-in-law, killed Kaholo Iolani, but Josh Fong, the sound engineer, killed Isabel West, the singer's personal assistant? When you said she was sleeping with Sangster, I would have figured the wife as the killer."

Vanessa swallowed a bit of chicken and licked her fingers, conscious of keeping her paperwork clean. "She knew he was fooling around, but she was sleeping with Josh Fong, herself. So she didn't have much motive against Isabel. From what I can tell about these folk singers, open marriages are pretty standard."

"But what was Paula's motive for killing Kaholo?" Terakawa asked. "And don't tell me it was the drugs. He's been a user for decades, and she knew it. Why would she suddenly go over the edge?"

Vanessa took another bite of delicious Hawaiian chicken. Chewing, she nodded toward the screen to signal that she was going to explain the whole thing. After swallowing and wiping her mouth with a rough paper towel. "Paula killed Kaholo because he tried to kill her husband, Jeffrey. It was Kaholo who shot at us that morning by the heiau. He aimed that antique shotgun-pistol at Jeffrey, but missed. I don't suppose it's easy to hit a target without a lot of practice with a weapon like that."

"What was that gun again?" Kaimi asked.

"A LeMat revolver, which had a second barrel and chamber for firing buckshot," said Lani. "I did a little research into it. It's a fascinating weapon made for the South in the Civil War. It's a big pistol combined with a small shotgun."

"Sounds like you're a real fan," Terakawa said.

Lani took another bite of papaya salad. "It's an interesting weapon, but I'll stay with my Glock."

Terakawa put down his plate. "You know, this is a first for me—having two partners working together on the same case. Well, ex-partner and current partner, that is." He picked up a bottle of water and guzzled half of it in one shot.

Vanessa continued with the story, annoyed at the interruption. "Anyway, Kaholo shot at Jeffrey, but missed, because he had seen Jeffrey arguing with his father at the heiau. He was the one who found Steven the next morning, and must have figured that the son killed the father for his money."

"But then, why did Fong kill Isabel West?"

Vanessa found a wet wipe in the bag from the

chicken shack and wiped her fingers carefully. "Josh Fong was actually Lahn Ngo, a Vietnamese national with a long rap sheet in Vietnam and California," she said, pointing to the printout of Ngo's record. "He learned sound recording in jail, and dreamed of being a big music producer. But in the meantime, he was still wholesaling drugs in Maui. Marijuana and, more recently, opioids. That's what the boat was for. And he had plans to increase his role in the Maui opioid market.

"He had been working legitimately for Steven Sangster, recording Kathryn Sangster, as well as the early work on the songs Steven intended for Erica Harrison. When Sangster died, he saw an opportunity. He stole the new songs, copied them onto a USB thumb drive—I'm sure we'll find backups soon—and erased all the other copies from the servers in the studio and anywhere else. He couldn't do anything about the samples Steven had sent earlier to Erica Harrison, of course.

"With Sangster dead, Ngo planned to sell the new songs to another singer, who could pass them off as his own.

"But Isabel West noticed that the new songs, the good ones, were missing and she confronted Ngo about them. So he killed her. When both the FBI and the Maui PD came to investigate a second death, on top of Sangster's and the shot at us, Ngo got spooked and tried to run. But that's when he was killed by Gilmour."

"And what was Gilmour's angle in this?"

Kaimi asked, cleaning his hands.

Lani took this question. "Gilmour was dirty. He's the main opioid distributor in this part of Maui. According to Steinberg—not the most reliable witness, but the only one we have at the moment—Ngo found a new source of opioids from Asia. Maybe he thought he could use his boat to help import the pills from the new source. I don't know. But the idea of losing a dealer network in Hana made Gilmour mad, so he killed Fong. I mean, Ngo."

King tried to sum up the situation. "Let me see if I got this straight. Jeffrey Sangster gets his father so worked up, he has a heart attack and dies."

"That's what the medical examiner's report concludes," said Vanessa, pointing to the report on the desk.

"But Kaholo, Sangster's oldest friend, sees it happen and thinks that the son did it deliberately. So he tries to kill Jeffrey with an antique gun, but misses."

"He chose the antique because he knew it would throw off the investigators," said Lani. "We were looking for a modern shotgun, not an antique pistol with a shotgun hidden in the middle."

"Josh Fong, or Lahn Ngo, sees an opportunity, and steals the new songs to try to sell them to some lowlife hack singer," King continued. "And when Isabel catches him, he kills her."

"That's about it," Lani said.

"But Fong, who's really Ngo, is dealing in marijuana and opioids, and when he tries to screw his supplier, that supplier kills *him*."

"So far, so good," said Vanessa.

"Meanwhile, Paula Sangster figures out that it was Kaholo who shot at her husband, so she kills him to protect her family. Like a mother bear or something."

"Yeah, she's pretty ferocious, all right," Vanessa said.

Terakawa popped the rest of the huli huli chicken in his mouth. Chewing, he said around the food "See, partner? Where would you be without me to figure things out for you? You're good at gathering evidence, but putting it all together in a narrative, well, you just can't beat me for that."

He dodged, laughing, when Vanessa threw an empty water bottle. "Just for that, you can organize those evidence reports. I'm exhausted. It's been a long day dealing with music stars."

Terakawa came up to her and wrapped a long, sinewy arm around her shoulders. "No problem. You go get cleaned up. In the two years we've worked together, I don't think I've ever seen you this dirty, and I gotta say, I'm getting close to a workplace violation." He winked, and Vanessa shrugged his arm off her shoulders.

As she left the station for her hotel, she noticed she was still wearing Kathryn Sangster's borrowed sweat clothes. She repeated her promise to herself.

Next time I come to Hana, it's strictly hiking clothes.

Chapter 22:
Loose ends

Perry was sitting on the bed when Vanessa opened the door to her hotel room, typing on a laptop computer. He looked up and smiled, closing the lid as she closed the door.

"How did you get in here?" she asked, dropping her shoulder bag on the little desk.

"I have my ways."

"Stop saying that! Really, Perry, the things you do to get close to me could constitute felonies individually, and add up to something pretty close to stalking."

"Stalking?" He stood, opening his arms the way he did for a hug. "Don't you think that's a little extreme? All I did was take some time after a work conference to be with the woman I love."

He stepped closer and then all she could see were his deep brown eyes. Those same eyes she had fallen in love with so many years ago.

Those same eyes that had looked up at her from under her roommate's naked chest. She stepped back. "That's very nice. But I'm working."

"You solved the case. I saw the local cops arresting people."

"I still have a report to write."

"When does Miller Time start for FBI agents?"

"In about an hour, when I finish this report."
Damn. I really can't stay mad at him when he looks at me like that. "Look, why don't you go down to the restaurant. Order us something really good and have it ready in an hour when I'm ready here."

"We could have room service."

"Fine," Vanessa answered as she took her tablet out of her bag, but she was not listening. She fired up the secure reporting app and sat at the little writing desk as the app opened. She typed in a summary of the past two days, attaching photo evidence and recordings of interviews. She didn't pay attention as Perry pored over the menus.

"You've always loved seafood," he said.

"Okay," Vanessa said without hearing Perry.

Perry left, but Vanessa barely registered the door closing, or when Perry came back almost an hour later with two bottles of wine. "This is much better than anything on the menu."

"Good," she answered without looking up from her tablet.

Perry bustled around the room, setting up a table for two and moving lamps around. Vanessa concentrated on her report.

Exactly one hour after Vanessa started, there was a knock on the door. Perry opened it for the room service waiter, who pushed in a cart covered with silver domes, glasses, cutlery and a candle.

Vanessa didn't look up as Perry tipped the waiter and closed the door, not even when he uncorked one of the bottles and put a full glass in front of her.

"Quitting time," he said, holding a glass of his own.

Vanessa looked up at him, then tore her eyes from his before he could work that old spell again. "Thanks, but I'm not quite done."

"Five more minutes, to make up for the distractions I've caused." He went to the balcony to look at the ocean under the dark, but clear sky.

Vanessa kept typing, but her concentration was broken. She typed in a completely uninspired closing and only after hitting "Send" did she realize she had copied it from the one Alan Terakawa had contributed to their last joint report. "Damn," she muttered.

Perry took the tablet away and closed the cover. "You're done. The sun is down and you're now off the clock."

Vanessa stood. "Don't tell me what to do. I'm a federal agent." She reached not for the tablet, but for the glass of wine. She sipped, her eyes closing. "That's wonderful. What is it?"

"It's a Chablis. About the only good French wine I could find in Hawaii. It was unbelievably overpriced, too."

"You know, there are good wines from California and Australia that probably cost less because they don't have to be shipped so far."

"Yah, but no one makes wine like the French. Am I wrong?"

Vanessa closed her eyes and sipped again. He wasn't wrong.

"Come sit down," he said, gesturing to the miniature hotel dining table he had set with two places, the bottle of wine and a burning candle.

Vanessa sat as Perry removed the chrome platters. Under each was a thick salmon steak on a bed of vegetables. "Looks great." They dug in to a symphony of seafood, Asian and local Hawaiian flavors.

They chatted about the food, the wine, the beauty of Maui and the comfort of the hotel, about their parents. Finally, though, Vanessa had to move the conversation to the serious level.

"Look, I appreciate that you came to see me. I really do," she began. "And I appreciate your help on this case. And of course, I *know* you'll keep everything you saw and heard about this case confidential. But if you're trying to rekindle a romance, it's going to take more than a surprise visit every couple of months."

"What—are you asking me to move in with you?" Perry paused, fork in hand, leaning across the table to lock those rich, soft brown eyes on her again.

Vanessa took another swallow of wine and choked a little. When she recovered, she carefully looked at him, but not into his eyes.

"What I'm saying is, I'm willing to try, too. But I want to take it slow. And I want you to stop interrogating and manipulating my parents into giving you information about where I am."

"All they told me is that you were assigned to the Maui resident office for a while. And I really did have a conference in Hawaii. So it wasn't that far out of my way. Not that that would have been a problem."

"Why is it that you have so many conferences in Hawaii?"

"Hey—if you could choose anywhere in the U.S.A. to have a conference, why wouldn't you choose Hawaii?"

Vanessa nodded. "Good point. So, about going slow. Can you do that?"

This time, Perry caught her eyes and held them. Vanessa found she was holding her breath. After a short eternity, he nodded lazily, tilting his head to the side. "Slow. Yah. I can do that."

Vanessa's gaze roved from Perry's eyes, to his mouth, to his dimpled chin, down his taut neck to his broad shoulders. His big, wide hand lightly held a fork, filled with delicious salmon. He reached across the table toward her. Vanessa remembered what his long, strong fingers could do to her.

She wondered whether she could follow her own rule about going slow.

The end

Thank you,

for reading this Hawaiian Storm mystery.

If you liked it, would you consider writing a review on Amazon and/or Goodreads? This will not only help boost the book, it will also help other readers like yourself who are looking for a good read.

And if you liked this book, you can find more of my work at my website, ScottBuryAuthor.com/ (http://ScottBuryAuthor.com). There you can sign up to get my email newsletter, *Forewords*, for advance information on new books and other projects. I promise never to spam you or give your personal information to anyone else. And as a further thank you, you'll receive a free e-book.

Thanks to author Toby Neal for getting me involved in writing Hawaii-set mysteries, to beta readers and especially my wife, Roxanne, for their insights and saving my bacon from a couple of pretty embarrassing mistakes.

I also have to thank my family, my wife, Roxanne, and my two mighty sons, Evan and Nicolas, for being them.

About the author

Scott Bury is a journalist, editor and novelist based in Ottawa, Canada. After more than 20 years of writing for magazines and newspapers like *Macworld*, the *Financial Post, Applied Arts*, the *Ottawa Citizen* and Graphic *Arts Monthly*, he turned to his first writing love, fiction. He published a children's story, "Sam, the Strawb Part" in 2011 and donated all the proceeds to an autism charity. Later, he published a short story for grown ups that might fall into the "urban paranormal" category, called "Dark Clouds."

The Bones of the Earth, a historical fantasy, came out in 2012. The second book in this Dark Age series, *The Children of the Seventh Son*, released in late 2020.

One Shade of Red, an erotic romantic spoof of the inexplicable bestseller, *Fifty Shades of Grey*, hit the shelves in 2013.

The Eastern Front Trilogy tells the true story of Maurice Bury, a Canadian drafted into the USSR's Red Army in 1941, just in time to face the German invasion of the Soviet Union in Operation

Barbarossa. It comprises *Army of Worn Soles* (2014), *Under the Nazi Heel* (2016) and *Walking Out of War* (2017).

In 2018, he launched the new Wine Country Mystery series with *Wildfire*.

In 2015 and 2016, he was invited to contribute to three Kindle Worlds, a project that was cancelled in 2018. He wrote seven titles for them.

In 2018, Scott Bury began publishing the Hawaiian Storm mystery series, with *Torn Roots* and then the Christmas-themed *Palm Trees & Snowflakes*. *Dead Man Lying* is the third book in this series.

In between writing books and blog posts, Scott helped to found an author's cooperative publishing venture, Independent Authors International. He is also President of an authors' professional association, BestSelling Reads.

You can find out more about Scott Bury and contact him through his website, www.writtenword.ca, his blog, Written Words, and on Twitter @ScottTheWriter.

Books by Scott Bury

Sam, the Strawb Part

Dark Clouds (The Witch's Child series)

The Dark Age series:
Initiation Rites (*The Bones of the Earth,* Part 1)
The Bones of the Earth (Book 1)
The Children of the Seventh Son (Book 2)

One Shade of Red

The *Eastern Front Trilogy*:
Army of Worn Soles
Under the Nazi Heel
Walking Out of War

The Hawaiian Storm series
Torn Roots
Palm Trees & Snowflakes
Dead Man Lying

Wine Country mysteries
Wildfire

Find them all on Scott Bury's website, ScottBuryAuthor.com

www.ingramcontent.com/pod-product-compliance
Lightning Source LLC
Chambersburg PA
CBHW060151180626
46813CB00007B/2698

* 9 7 8 1 9 8 7 8 4 6 2 8 7 *